W9-DDU-634

May, 2010

The Sword & the Pen

INDIANA HISTORICAL SOCIETY PRESS
INDIANAPOLIS 2005

The Sword & the Pen

A Life of Lew Wallace

RAY E. BOOMHOWER

© 2005 Indiana Historical Society Press. All rights reserved.

This book is a publication of the
Indiana Historical Society Press
450 West Ohio Street
Indianapolis, Indiana 46202-3269 USA
www.indianahistory.org
Telephone orders 1-800-447-1830
Fax orders 1-317-234-0562
Online Orders @ shop.indianahistory.org

Photo credits for title page: (left) Indiana Historical Society, Lew Wallace Collection, M292;
(right) Courtesy the Lilly Library, Indiana University, Bloomington, Indiana.

Portions of this book previously appeared in the winter 1993 issue of
Traces of Indiana and Midwestern History.

Made possible with support from the Lilly Endowment, Inc.

Library of Congress Cataloging-in-Publication Data

Boomhower, Ray E., 1959-
    The sword and the pen : a life of Lew Wallace / Ray E. Boomhower.
        p. cm.
    Includes bibliographical references (p. 147).
    ISBN 0-87195-185-1 (casebound : alk. paper)
1. Wallace, Lew, 1827-1905—Juvenile literature. 2. Generals—United States—Biography—Juvenile
literature. 3. United States. Army—Biography—Juvenile literature. 4. Authors, American—19th
century—Biography—Juvenile literature. I. Indiana Historical Society.
II. Title.
    E467.1.W2B66 2005
    978.9'04'092--dc22
                                                                                    2005049291

Printed in Canada

For Megan, who made it all possible.

"The secret to success is work! work! work!"
—*Lew Wallace*

Contents

Acknowledgments

For anyone writing a biography of a famous subject, there are guides who offer assistance along the way. For their help in gathering research materials on Lew Wallace's life and times, I thank the staff of the Indiana Historical Society Press's Wallace Papers Project, including Doug Clanin, Suzanne Bellamy, and Lucinda Barnhart. IHS Press editors Paula Corpuz and Rachel Popma offered sound advice on improving the book before its publication. As she has on all my books, my wife, Megan McKee, offered her suggestions on my work. Lew had Susan; I have Megan.

My thanks as well to those who helped with obtaining photographs for the book: Susan Sutton at the Society's William Henry

Smith Memorial Library; Saundra Taylor at the Lilly Library at Indiana University; and Cinnamon Catlin-Legutko at the General Lew Wallace Study and Museum in Crawfordsville, Indiana.

Pat Prather at Dean Johnson Design in Indianapolis has once again used her considerable talents on the design of the book. Thanks to Pat for making Lew look so good.

The book would not have been possible without the substantial financial support of the Lilly Endowment, Inc. My thanks to the Endowment for its continued aid to Indiana's past.

A drawing of Major General Lew Wallace on his horse John during the Civil War.

INDIANA HISTORICAL SOCIETY M0450

Chapter 1

Dreams *of* Glory

F or Lew Wallace of Indiana, the chance for greatness had finally
come.

The free and legal election of a Republican—Abraham Lincoln
of Illinois—to the presidency in November 1860 had caused many
southern states to threaten to withdraw from the Union. Once
free, they planned to form a nation dedicated to preserving and
spreading the institution of slavery.

A month after Lincoln's victory, South Carolina became the
first state to secede. Other southern states soon followed. In
February 1861 Jefferson Davis, a former U.S. senator, had been
named the new president of the Confederate States of America.

Although politicians on both sides had attempted to avoid bloodshed, they could not reach agreement on a compromise. At 4:30 in the morning on April 12, 1861, Confederate forces started the American Civil War by firing on Fort Sumter, a Union military base located outside the entrance to the harbor at Charleston, South Carolina. Just two days later, after suffering severe damage from four thousand shells, the federal forces surrendered. The American flag came down, and the Confederacy's new Stars and Bars banner flew over the fort.

The attack on Fort Sumter caused those in the North to quickly rally to protect the Union. President Lincoln called for 75,000 volunteers to enlist for ninety days to meet the national emergency. Each state worked to fill its quota of soldiers called for by the president.

The state of Indiana planned to fill the ranks of six regiments, about 4,600 men. "Soldiers, or good men willing to be converted into soldiers for the emergency," noted one Indiana newspaper, "seem to spring up out of the ground, eager to protect the flag and conquer the peace." Governor Oliver P. Morton, a Republican and strong supporter of the president, named Lew Wallace to serve as the state's adjutant general. As part of his new job, Wallace worked to organize the Hoosier volunteers into a fighting force. Wallace's pay for this important work: $100 a year.

Although he had served as an officer with an Indiana regiment during the American war with Mexico in the late 1840s, Wallace had not been involved in a major fight. This son of a former Indiana governor had seen the dead left behind on the battlefield. But Wallace had never been at the front ranks facing enemy forces, hearing the screams of shot and shell.

From an early age, however, Wallace had romantic dreams of winning glory and fame. His father, David Wallace, had graduated from the U.S. Military Academy at West Point, the college that provided America with officers for its army. Among Lew Wallace's earliest memories was seeing the uniform his father wore while a student at West Point. The "shining bullet-buttons of the coat captured my childish fancy," he said.

Young Lew also remembered the time when his family was living in Covington, Indiana, located near the border with Illinois. Word had spread that the town might face attack from hostile Native Americans under the leadership of Chief Black Hawk. With his military experience, David Wallace helped to organize the local men into a fighting force to protect the community. Seeing his father lead the local militia inspired then five-year-old Lew Wallace to become a soldier. "My noblest dream of life has been one of fame," he noted in his journal.

Instead of concentrating on his schoolwork, Wallace spent his time in class filling his slate with drawings of soldiers fighting. These battle scenes included officers on horseback swinging long swords and wearing tall, feathery hats.

His interest in the military continued even after he left school. While working in the county clerk's office in Indianapolis as a young man, Wallace joined a local military company known as the Marion Rifles. He later grew tired of studying law in his father's office and volunteered for service in the Mexican War. After his safe return to Indiana, Wallace finished his studies and earned a license to practice law. He never enjoyed being an attorney, later calling it "the most detestable of human occupations."

Opening a law practice in Covington, Wallace also served as state prosecuting attorney and won election to the Indiana senate. Yet, through all of these activities, he continued to be fascinated by the military. At night, Wallace studied manuals and books on how to lead soldiers. While living in Crawfordsville, he organized a militia unit called the Montgomery Guards and led them in drills.

After reading a magazine article on the colorful uniforms and dashing exploits of the Zouaves, a French Algerian army unit, Wallace outfitted his men in their style of uniform. He also trained his recruits in the quick march and commando strategies used by the Zouaves. Wallace enjoyed his experience as commander and believed he and his men might soon have to put their practice to the test as the question of slavery threatened to tear the country apart.

Wallace therefore was ready when fighting started between the North and South with the shelling of Fort Sumter. In his autobiography he said that at the time he expected a long war filled with "opportunities for distinction not in the least inconsistent with patriotism." As the Hoosier State's adjutant general, Wallace worked feverishly to organize the volunteers streaming into Indianapolis into regiments of determined fighting men.

Just four days after President Lincoln's call for six regiments from Indiana, Wallace had managed to raise twice the number needed. "They were farmer boys, apprentice lads, leaders in villages, heads of public school," Wallace said of the volunteers, "with here a city-born, and there a college-bred, and nearly all of them in the morning of life." All had responded to Wallace's call to rally to the flag of their country.

With his task complete, Wallace resigned his post and, with the blessing of Governor Morton, took command of the Eleventh Indiana Volunteer Infantry Regiment. Now a colonel, Wallace contracted to have his troops outfitted in the Zouave uniform of caps with visors, baggy pants, and narrow jackets, just as he had done with the Montgomery Guards. His "love of military life" and flair for the dramatic showed itself in a thrilling event that inspired citizens throughout the North.

In early May 1861 Wallace marched his troops out of camp to the statehouse, where women from Terre Haute and Indianapolis presented the regiment with two flags—its colors—before a large, cheering crowd. Observing the ceremony that day, Catharine

The Eleventh Indiana Volunteer Infantry Regiment, under the command of Wallace, swears to "Remember Buena Vista!" before a cheering crowd in Indianapolis, May 1861.

Merrill, a Hoosier historian and writer, described Colonel Wallace as "very American in appearance" with a "deep, flashing eye, straight, shining black hair, and erect figure."

Addressing his rookie soldiers, the thirty-four-year-old Wallace reminded them that at the Battle of Buena Vista during the Mexican War, Jefferson Davis, now president of the traitorous Confederacy, had unfairly charged that a regiment of Indiana troops had been cowards. Davis had passed along the charge to his father-in-law, General Zachary Taylor.

Wallace had his troops kneel and promise to wipe out the disgrace cast on the state by Davis. The regiment took as its motto "Remember Buena Vista!" The dramatic scene, which according to one newspaper "filled hundreds of manly eyes with tears," caught the nation's attention. The influential magazine *Harper's Weekly* produced a full-page illustration of the event for its readers.

IHS, C5187

The Eleventh Indiana soon experienced battle, what Civil War troops called "seeing the elephant." In June 1861 Wallace and his men surprised Confederate forces in Romney, Virginia, driving them from the town and winning the praise of northern newspapers starved for good news from the battlefront. Moving to the western theater of the war, the regiment participated in successful campaigns in Tennessee under the leadership of General Ulysses S. Grant.

Battle flags of the Eleventh Indiana from the Civil War.

IHS, LEW WALLACE COLLECTION, M292

Success in battle soon brought honors to Wallace. In March 1862 he received promotion to the rank of major general, the highest then available. "My greatest personal satisfaction," Wallace said of his early days in the war, "was due to the discovery of the fact that in the confusion and feverish excitement of real battle, I could think." The road to further fame and glory seemed clear. All that changed, however, at the bloody Battle of Shiloh.

On the morning of April 6, 1862, rebel troops under the command of General Albert Sidney Johnston surprised Grant's Union forces and pushed their blue-coated foes all the way to the banks of the Tennessee River. Stationed miles away from the initial action, Wallace finally received an order from Grant to come to the aid of his panicked troops. Controversy still rages today about the exact orders Wallace received. He proceeded to take his command on a long, tough march—at one point finding himself at the rear of the Confederate army—that put his force out of action on the battle's first day.

Wallace and his men, joined by additional troops brought by General Don Carlos Buell, played an important role in driving the rebels from the field on the second day of fighting. When the smoke cleared from the battlefield, dead and wounded men from both sides lay as far as the eye could see. Grant noted that "it would have been possible to walk across the clearing in any direction stepping on dead bodies without a foot touching the ground." Of the 100,000 men who fought, 3,477 were dead—a number greater than all of the country's battle deaths in the American Revolution, War of 1812, and Mexican War combined.

Although Shiloh was a victory for the Union, the large casualties shocked the nation. The battle cost Grant his command for a time, as General Henry Halleck relieved him. Although Wallace continued to lead his troops, there were rumors that he had been lost on the battle's first day. His impatience with being out of the action and his confidence in his skill as a fighter also cost him dearly. Halleck, a graduate of West Point whom Wallace had criticized, believed amateur officers such as Wallace were unfit to lead troops.

Back home in Indiana on leave, Wallace learned from Governor Morton that he had been placed "on the shelf," dismissed from active service in the Union army. Wallace returned home to Crawfordsville to await whatever fate had in store for him. In late summer 1862 northern military leaders called him back into action to help bolster defenses around Cincinnati, Ohio, to thwart an expected Confederate assault. Wallace won the respect of the city's residents for his inspiring leadership, as he organized volunteers to build such strong defenses that the rebels decided to abandon their plans for an attack.

The "turning point," as Wallace termed it, in the rebirth of his military career came on March 12, 1864, when he received orders from the government to take command of the Eighth Army Corps, which was headquartered in Baltimore, Maryland. Four months later, Wallace led a small force of Union soldiers at Monocacy Junction in a desperate attempt to stop a large Confederate army from capturing Washington, D.C., the Union capital.

Although defeated at what came to be called the Battle of Monocacy, Wallace had delayed the Confederates' march on Washington by a full day, giving Grant, by then the North's leading general, enough time to send reinforcements to successfully beat back any Confederate strike on the nation's capital.

Following the end of the Civil War in 1865, Wallace continued to find ways to contribute to his state and country. He was on the military court that tried those involved with the assassination of President Lincoln. Wallace aided Mexican freedom fighters in their struggles to rid their country of its French ruler Louis Napoléon. Appointed as governor of the New Mexico Territory during a bloody period in that area's history, Wallace had to deal with such famous outlaws as Billy the Kid. During his service as U.S. minister to Turkey, he won the respect of its feared ruler, Sultan Abdul Hamid II.

All of these impressive achievements, however, failed to heal for Wallace the "old wound" of the Battle of Shiloh. "Shiloh and its slanders! Will the world ever acquit me of them?" Wallace wrote his wife, Susan. "If I were guilty I would not feel them so keenly."

The stain on Wallace's military career, however, has faded away over the years as he won his "noblest dream" of fame through another occupation: writing. His historical novel Ben-Hur: A Tale of the Christ sold millions of copies throughout the world. Wallace had developed a love of books and reading at an early age. During his father's years as governor, he discovered the books available at the statehouse's library. He eagerly read the works of such early American writers as James Fenimore Cooper and Washington Irving.

Wallace had little luck with most Hoosier teachers, who punished his frequent absences with beatings. At age thirteen, however,

Wallace was sent by his father to a school in Centerville, Indiana, taught by Professor Samuel K. Hoshour. "Professor Hoshour was the first to observe a glimmer of writing capacity in me," said Wallace. The professor had Wallace read great English writers such as William Shakespeare and the New Testament from the Bible, including the story of the birth of Jesus Christ. "Little did I dream then what those few verses were to bring me—that out of them Ben-Hur was one day to be evoked," said Wallace.

Writing came naturally to Wallace. He began writing his first novel in the late 1840s while working in the Marion County clerk's office copying records. Reading a history of early Mexico, he was inspired to write a book about the Spanish conquest of the Aztec Empire. Finally published in the fall of 1873, Wallace's book, *The Fair God*, benefited greatly from his personal travels in Mexico and his extensive research into the country's history. One London newspaper went as far to praise the book as "one of the most powerful historical novels that we have ever read."

Wallace's next work won a place for him in the country's literary history. *Ben-Hur* had its beginnings as early as December 1873, when Wallace wrote his sister about doing research on his new book at the Library of Congress in Washington, D.C.

The Hoosier writer received an added boost to his efforts a few years later through a chance conversation with Robert G. Ingersoll, a famous agnostic (one who

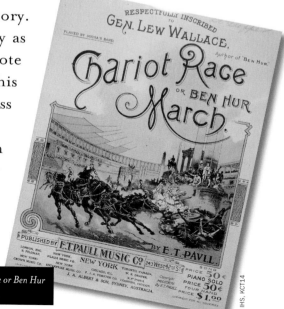

Sheet music for the E. T. Paull Music Company's song "Chariot Race or Ben Hur March" in honor of Wallace's famous book Ben-Hur.

IHS, KCT14

Wallace and his grandson, Lew Wallace Jr., at the author's study in Crawfordsville, Indiana.

COLIN INDIANAPOLIS COLLECTION IMAGE, IHS

doubts there is a God). During a train trip to a soldiers' reunion in Indianapolis, the two veterans of the Civil War sat together and talked about "God, heaven, life hereafter, Jesus Christ, and his divinity," Wallace recalled.

Although Wallace had never been a member of any church and "was not in the least influenced by religious sentiment," he was troubled by his talk with Ingersoll and resolved to study the matter "if only for the gratification there might be in having convictions of one kind or another."

Realizing that Christians might protest a fictional story with Jesus Christ as a main character, Wallace told Christ's story through Judah Ben-Hur, a Jewish noble, and his struggles with his Roman friend and rival Messala. Wallace wrote the book whenever he found time in his busy schedule, including on summer days while sitting in the shade of a beech tree at his home in Crawfordsville and during his days as governor of the New Mexico Territory.

Published by Harper and Brothers on November 12, 1880, *Ben-Hur* sold slowly at first, but sales gradually grew by leaps and bounds until it became a sensational success. Readers across the country and around the world were moved and thrilled by Wallace's romantic tale, especially the exciting chariot race between Ben-Hur and Messala. "It seems now that when I sit down finally in the old man's gown and slippers, helping the cat to keep the fireplace warm," said Wallace, "I shall look back upon Ben-Hur as my best performance."

As years passed, the book remained popular. Towns were named after Ben-Hur, and the novel also sparked the creation of a national fraternal organization that later became a life insurance company. In 1889 the book was made into a stage play and later several motion pictures were produced.

The most famous film made from the book came in 1959 and starred Charlton Heston as Ben-Hur and Stephen Boyd as Messala.

The movie won eleven Academy Awards and has been shown on television numerous times, especially during Easter. The film also won an honor from the American Film Institute in 1998 as one of the hundred greatest movies of all time.

Ben-Hur's huge sales brought Wallace and his wife financial security. The money gave Wallace the ability to build what he called "a pleasure-house for my soul." He wanted a place where he could "write and . . . think of nothing else. I want to bury myself in a den of books." Completed in 1898 in Crawfordsville, the structure, which came to be known as the Lew Wallace Study, is today a museum that is dedicated to Wallace's life and work.

Wallace had only a few years to enjoy his study. He died at his Crawfordsville home on February 15, 1905. Before his final illness, the Civil War veteran had noted the death of a fellow soldier by saying: "He is but a day's march ahead of us; we shall overtake him soon."

Lew Wallace should be remembered as one of the most colorful and important figures in Indiana's history. He could be impatient and boastful at times, but Wallace played a leading role in the country's military, political, diplomatic, and literary affairs during the nineteenth century. A man of many talents, a true "Renaissance man," he dreamed of glory and lived a life full of adventures, triumphs, and tragedies. Through it all, he firmly believed in his own abilities. The possibility of failure never prevented him from testing himself. "May a man tell what he can do until he tries?" Wallace asked. "That, I take it, is the soul of the Americanism which has made us a peculiar people."

Chapter 2

An Indiana Boyhood

Brookville, Indiana, is located near the Whitewater River in the eastern part of the state, near its border with Ohio. Founded in 1808 by Amos Butler and Jesse Thomas, the community became the seat of government for Franklin County three years later. It also became the home of the federal land office where settlers coming to the young state could buy property cheaply from the government. They then could work to turn the rich soil into prosperous farms. In his family's sturdy, two-story brick home in Brookville, Lewis Wallace was born on April 10, 1827. Lew, as he came to be called, was the second of four sons raised by David and Esther French Test Wallace.

Lew possessed the same black eyes as his brothers, but as a child he had light-colored hair with a thick thatch that fell over his forehead. Lew expressed pride in his father, who had graduated from the U.S. Military Academy at West Point in 1821. David had received his appointment to the academy through his father's friendship with one of pioneer Indiana's leading figures: William Henry Harrison, the hero of the Battle of Tippecanoe.

David Wallace, Lew's father and Indiana's sixth governor.

IHS, LEW WALLACE COLLECTION, M292

After serving for a time as a mathematics teacher at the military academy, David Wallace settled in Brookville. He studied law with Judge Miles Eggleston and became a lawyer. On November 10, 1824, he married Esther French Test, the daughter of a judge and congressman.

Writing about his father, Lew remembered him as "a man of noble presence in the slender elegance of youth, straight and tall, with a well-shaped head set squarely on his shoulders." Known as a spellbinding speaker, David turned to politics, winning election to the Indiana General Assembly as a member of the Whig Party and also serving two terms as lieutenant governor, the state's second highest office.

In 1832 David moved the family to Covington, Indiana, located along the Wabash River near the border with Illinois, to go into business with his brother. The family traveled to its new home by

14

horse and carriage over the state's rough roads. During the journey, two of the children, John and Lew, became ill with scarlet fever. Lew survived but his brother died. Looking back on his illness later in life, Lew could only remember being made to drink scalding hot cups of saffron tea and "the large brown eyes of my mother swimming in tears."

Lew quickly came to enjoy Covington. The town sat on an elevated plain and had on its north, east, and west sides large stands of forests that Lew could explore to his heart's content. The nearby Wabash River also impressed him with its size and opportunities for adventure.

Lew made friends with a man who operated a ferry that took travelers back and forth across the river. Although still small in size, Lew helped the man with the ferry. When customers were rare, he fished for minnows in the river. Fishing became a hobby that Lew enjoyed the rest of his life. Whenever he had to forget his troubles, or simply wanted to relax, he grabbed a pole and headed out for a day's fishing.

Shortly after settling into its new home, the Wallace family suffered a scare. Sauk Indians under Chief Black Hawk had killed two settlers in Illinois and were expected to make an attack on Covington any day. David Wallace, with his military background, organized a militia company to meet the threat and drilled them on the town square. The activity made a big impression on the young Lew, who soon dreamed of becoming a soldier and marching off to war behind his country's flag.

At the age of six, Lew began attending the local one-room brick schoolhouse. The lessons taught by the stern Irish teacher, however, failed to attract the boy's attention. He much preferred to be outdoors, fishing in the Wabash River or exploring and hunting in the nearby forests. Lew also discovered he had a talent for drawing. He soon spent most of his school days drawing portraits of his classmates and scenes of soldiers in action on the battlefield. For not paying attention to his studies, Lew suffered numerous whippings from his teacher, who "made a playground for his practice" on the boy's back.

Trouble at school also caused difficulty for Lew at home. He endured spankings from his father for his misbehavior. Hoping to keep him at home and out of mischief, Lew's mother resorted to the "annoying" punishment of tying her son to the bedpost and dressing him in women's clothes. Her tears, however, were the most powerful weapon Lew's mother used in getting her son to behave. His good conduct, however, lasted only a short time. Then the "unconquerable part" of Lew's nature took hold, and he returned to skipping school and exploring the woods and fields he loved.

His first teacher did give Lew one valuable lesson—he taught him to read. The first book Lew read involved a young man from New England who ran away to sea and narrowly escaped being sold into slavery by pirates. "The craving it awoke," he later said of his passion for reading, "is not yet satisfied."

Lew's mother discovered that the only way she could keep control of her wandering child was to give him a book. She introduced him to *The Scottish Chiefs*, an exciting account of the lives of William Wallace and Robert the Bruce of Scotland. Lew and his brother William were so thrilled by these tales of old that they and three schoolmates turned them into a play and "went to war with the haughty English." He also became fascinated with a book on geography. The book's maps and pictures of other countries and people opened the world to the young Hoosier.

On July 14, 1834, while David Wallace was in New York on business, Esther Wallace died after a brief illness. Years later, Lew had only faint memories of his mother, remembering her "eyes, large, sparkling, and deeply brown. They follow me yet." For the next three years, Lew and his brothers lived at the home of a neighbor.

With his father often away from home on business or for his political career, Lew turned instead for comfort to his older brother, William, who became his hero.

The two were parted, however, when William journeyed to Crawfordsville to attend the preparatory department at what would become Wabash College. "The separation nearly broke my heart," Lew said. Learning that an uncle would soon be going to Crawfordsville, the nine-year-old Lew waited along a road until his uncle came by on his horse. Lew stopped his uncle and asked him to take him to join his brother at college. The uncle agreed and dropped him off at the school's entrance.

When William finally appeared, he saw his scruffy young brother standing before him dressed in a straw hat with his pants rolled up to his knees and one toe tied with a large rag. The amused teachers at the college allowed Lew to attend class for a time. He spent a few weeks there before transferring to another school more suitable to his age in Crawfordsville.

FROM THE COLLECTIONS OF THE GENERAL LEW WALLACE STUDY AND MUSEUM, CRAWFORDSVILLE, INDIANA

Zerelda Wallace, Lew Wallace's stepmother.

17

David Wallace returned to Crawfordsville in 1836 with the Whig Party's nomination for governor of Indiana and a new wife, Zerelda Gray Sanders, the daughter of a successful doctor. (Later in life, she became a leading figure in the Woman's Christian Temperance Union's fight against liquor.) Although his new mother offered him nothing but kindness, Lew treated her with a "sulky and stubborn" manner. All that changed when he returned home sick after days spent tramping in the woods. "She put me to bed," Lew said, "and nursed me with infinite skill and tenderness. I had sense enough to know she was the savior of my life, and called her mother."

In the 1837 election for Indiana governor, David Wallace defeated his opponent, John Dumont, by approximately nine thousand votes and took office at a salary of $1,200 per year.

Taking over his duties as the Hoosier State's chief executive, David moved his family to Indianapolis, which had been named as the state capital in 1820. Over the years, the city had grown slowly, with one visitor saying in 1833 that he had never seen a community "so utterly forlorn as Indianapolis." The city's vacant downtown lots were filled with the stumps of trees, and horse-drawn wagons frequently became stuck in the muddy streets.

A view of the Indiana Statehouse at the time David Wallace served as governor of the nineteenth state.

There were signs of progress, however, as David began his term as governor. A new statehouse with a dome had been built in the early 1830s. The city's central location in the state made it a key stop for those traveling on the busy National Road. In 1836 the Indiana legislature had passed an act allowing the state to borrow millions of dollars to fund the building of canals, railroads, and roads. By 1837 four thousand people made Indianapolis their home.

For Lew, his new home offered a chance for a smoother life. This was due partly to his father's firm discipline, but also to his new stepmother, who kept the youngster "washed, combed, and well-clad." Zerelda even insisted that Lew attend church on Sunday. Instead of paying attention to the sermon, however, he turned his cap into a drawing tablet and began doodling on it sketches of the preacher and members of the congregation.

Resuming his wanderings, Lew also visited the studio of Jacob Cox, one of Indiana's most famous early artists. Inspired by the artist's work, Lew began to produce his own paintings and talked of earning a living from art. His father, however, lectured him on the foolishness of pursuing an occupation that offered little chance for financial success.

Although he reluctantly abandoned art as a profession, Lew continued to envy those who created artworks and continued to make sketches the rest of his life. He soon discovered a new outlet for his energies at the statehouse library. Entering the room for the first time, he stood in awe at the number of volumes filling the shelves. "Books everywhere, of all sizes, of all colors!" he remembered. "Had any one ever read them all?"

Lew spent the rest of the day examining the books on display and returned for days on end. In the library, he became drawn to the works of such American writers as Washington Irving and, especially, James Fenimore Cooper, author of the stirring novel *The Last of the Mohicans*. He also thrilled to the romantic tales of adventure written by Scottish novelist and poet Sir Walter Scott. "For months and months after that discovery my name figured on the receipt register of the library more frequently than any other," Lew said.

His fondness for reading, however, did not mean Lew did any better in school. He continued to skip classes whenever he could, including a twelve-day absence while his father was out of town in May 1840. Lew joined a large crowd traveling to the Tippecanoe battlefield to attend a rally for Whig Party presidential candidate William Henry Harrison. Hitching a ride on a wagon driven by a friendly Harrison supporter, Lew made it to the rally. "I candidly believe that no one of the multitude attending the convention saw or heard more of it than I did; for, once on the ground, I took no rest, neither did I sleep," he said.

David Wallace also supported Harrison, campaigning on behalf of the war hero during the election, which Harrison won. David, however, failed to win another term as governor. A financial panic that swept the nation in 1839 had halted work on the many improvement projects being built in the state and plunged Indiana deeply into debt.

The Whig Party decided not to renominate David as its candidate for governor. He later won election to the U.S. Congress, but was defeated in his attempt at another term in office. During the campaign, his opponent mocked him for giving tax money to help Samuel F. B. Morse with his telegraph invention. David had the last laugh, however. In 1858, when Indianapolis organized a huge celebration to mark the successful laying of a telegraph cable across the Atlantic Ocean, David gave the main speech.

David Wallace's political troubles were more than matched by the antics of his son Lew. Learning of a teacher in Centerville with a good reputation for helping troubled youths, the former governor sent his thirteen-year-old son there for schooling. The teacher, Professor Samuel K. Hoshour, treated Lew with "infinite patience" and even interested him in mathematics, a subject he had never before understood. The professor also became the first person "to observe a glimmer of writing capacity in me," Lew said.

The year he spent with Hoshour was the "turning point" in his life, according to Lew. The teacher introduced him to lectures by former president John Quincy Adams on speech, the works of William Shakespeare, and the story of the birth of Jesus Christ from the New Testament. "Were you to ask me," Hoshour advised the young man, "which of the rules is the most important, which comes nearest being the essence of the whole art, here it is: In writing, everything is to be sacrificed to clearness of expression—everything." Lew never forgot that lesson.

Upon his return to Indianapolis, Lew joined a local literary society. He wrote poems that were published in Indianapolis newspapers, including a tale called "The Travels of a Bed-bug," where the insect traveled from victim to victim before drinking itself to death. Lew even completed 250 pages of a romantic novel he titled "The Man at Arms: A Tale of the Tenth Century." He later misplaced the manuscript. "Even then," he said, "the importance to a writer of first discerning a body of readers possible of capture and then addressing himself to their tastes was a matter of instinct with me."

His dedication to his new craft did not mean that Lew had given up his habit of wandering wherever and whenever the spirit moved him. Inspired by the heroic tales of the Texans' fight for independence from Mexico, Lew and one of his classmates, Aquilla Cook, the son of the first statehouse librarian, decided to leave town and offer their services to the Texas navy.

The two boys set sail on a small boat down the White River in hopes of catching a flatboat bound for New Orleans. Unfortunately for the duo, they were caught by a police officer and a relative of Lew's about ten miles outside of Indianapolis.

Now sixteen years old,

Poster supporting the presidential campaign of William Henry Harrison in 1840.

IHS, BASS PHOTO COMPANY COLLECTION, P130

Lew, after his failed bid for a Texas adventure, described him-self as "unusually tall, thin" and having "an all-abiding confidence in myself." But Lew's father did not share his son's belief about having a successful future. One day, after breakfast, Lew met his father in his study in the family's Indianapolis home. Standing before the elder Wallace, Lew noticed him pulling a large bundle of papers wrapped with red tape from the drawer of a nearby table. The papers were receipts from the bills David had paid for all of his son's schooling through the years.

After Lew had read the papers, his father noted that if he died that night, his son's inheritance would support him for only a month. "I have struggled to give you and your brothers what, in my opinion, is better than money—education," said David. Express-ing his disappointment in Lew's previous behavior, his father told him from that day forward he would have to go out in the world and earn his own living. "I shall watch your course hopefully," he said. "That is all I have to say." Before Lew left the one-story, log home for the last time, except as a visitor, he and his father shook hands.

The decision by David Wallace to cut off his financial support for his son came as no surprise to Lew. He agreed that he had been given every chance to make good in school and thanked his father for his kindness. "He was a good man and patient; I had been a bad boy—that was all," said Lew. He recalled how his father had tried to share his love of literature with his sons, reading to them from Brit-ish magazines and from the works of such great writers as Thomas Macaulay, John Milton, Scott, and Shakespeare. "My education, such as it was," Lew later said, "is due to my father's library."

With his boyhood ended, Lew had to find a way to earn a liv-ing. He turned for help to a family friend, Robert S. Duncan, who ran the Marion County clerk's office and had been teaching law to Lew's brother William. Telling Duncan what had happened with his father, the young man asked for a job. Duncan gave him the task of copying official records—pleadings, orders, judgments, and dates of filing—at ten cents for every hundred words he wrote. By working from nine o'clock in the morning to five o'clock in the evening, Lew could write three thousand words a day and earn eighteen dollars a week.

Finding a job did not cure Lew's thirst for the outdoor life. When he received his first payment for work from Duncan, he paid rent for his room at a local boardinghouse and discovered he had eleven dollars left over. "The money made me restless and uneasy, and burned in my pocket," Lew remembered.

He took the money and bought a rifle. Duncan, one of the area's best shots, invited him to go hunting. When they re-

An 1854 view of the city of Indianapolis.

IHS, BASS PHOTO COMPANY COLLECTION

turned from the successful hunt, Duncan advised Lew that the next time he felt the need to go hunting, he should come to him first. "I saw in an instant that he understood the struggle upon me and was seeking to be helpful on my side," said Lew. He sat the gun aside and went back to work.

In the past, reading books had always helped Lew to relax. Copying large amounts of records all day meant that when he now looked upon pages from a once-favorite book, he became restless. Writing helped to ease his mind, but he wanted more. He set out to educate himself. At night, after his work in the clerk's office had been set aside, he studied.

After learning the rules of grammar, Lew looked for a subject to write about. He found it in a book from his father's library, a three-volume work by William Prescott titled *Conquest of Mexico*. The book told the exciting story of Hernando Cortés, Spanish explorer and soldier, and his battles with Montezuma II, the Aztec emperor and ruler of Mexico.

Prescott's tale of adventure, combat, and heroic deeds inspired Lew to write his own fictional tale of the conquest of Mexico (eventually published in 1873 under the title *The Fair God*). In doing research for his book, he investigated the geography of Mexico, learned the customs of the people who lived there, and even taught himself Spanish so he could read the stories of the conquistadors who fought beside Cortés. He worked on his book whenever he could find the time for the next thirty years of his life. Writing, however, took a back seat to Lew's childhood hopes for military glory.

Chapter 3

A Soldier's Life

At the age of sixteen, Lew Wallace had finally settled into a routine. He patiently copied records at the county clerk's office and continued to work on his historical novel about the conquest of Mexico. Wallace also found time to take dancing lessons from a traveling teacher, a Frenchman. The young man had not, however, forgotten his boyhood dreams of serving in battle.

At this time, Indianapolis was home to a successful military company called the City Greys, which was led by a graduate of the military academy at West Point. Most of the men who belonged to the Greys were middle-aged and were equipped with decent uniforms and guns. Wallace joined a new group called the Marion

Rifles. The ranks of the Rifles were filled with young men who were not yet old enough "to grow mustaches" and had to be content with a simple uniform of "a cotton hunting-shirt," noted Wallace, who was elected by the men as second sergeant.

The Greys and the Rifles became rivals, and the members of Wallace's company waited for a chance to get even with the Greys for insulting them with the nickname "Arabs" for their sloppy appearance. The two groups participated in a fake battle to mark the anniversary of Andrew Jackson's victory over the British at the Battle of New Orleans in 1812. In the excitement, the captain of the Rifles forgot to order retreat, as called for in the schedule of activities. Wallace and his men charged, shot one man with a blank cartridge, and took several prisoners. At the end of the day, Wallace and the Rifles cheered their victory until their throats were sore.

The thrill of battle "put a final finish upon the taste for military life by turning it into a genuine passion," said Wallace. He came upon a book on infantry tactics by American General Winfield Scott and for a time put everything aside in order to learn all he could about a soldier's duties.

By the time he turned eighteen, Wallace had grown tired of his job copying records in the clerk's office. He continued to work on his tale of Mexico, always carrying with him scraps of paper so he could write down ideas for his book as they came to him. Still, he wanted to do more with his life. His brother, William, had started to study law with their father, and Lew decided to join him. In those days, a person interested in becoming a lawyer could "read law" in a practicing attorney's office before taking exams and being admitted into the profession.

The routine paperwork of a lawyer's job did not attract him. Instead, Wallace became fascinated with the public part of the occupation—appearing in a courtroom and arguing a case for a client before a judge and jury. Also, becoming a lawyer often helped a person to enter the world of politics—always a popular pastime in Indiana. Wallace had experienced a taste of the political life while reporting on the Indiana legislature in 1844 for the *Indianapolis Daily Journal*. While working at the newspaper, he also earned money from legislators by helping them to write resolutions, bills, and other reports. He became "determined to take to the law."

For the next year, Wallace buried himself in his new occupation. During the day he studied law in his father's office. At night, he worked on his book. Whenever he needed money for clothes or rent, he returned to the county clerk's office and copied records. By the spring, he had learned enough law to defend clients in court for minor offenses. According to Wallace, he soon became a lawyer "of some local renown."

Wallace became less interested in becoming a lawyer as he learned of the growing tensions between the United States and Mexico. War seemed likely to break out at any moment. The Republic of Texas had won its independence from Mexico in 1836. Since then, there were many in Texas lobbying to join the United States. Those who opposed slavery, however, protested against the admission of a new state that allowed such a practice. Despite these objections, Texas entered the Union as a slave state during the administration of President James K. Polk, a Democrat who took office in 1844.

President Polk believed it was America's "Manifest Destiny" to expand westward, and he sought to gain new territory for the United States. The president used a dispute with Mexico over the southern border of Texas as a reason to send American troops to the region. Those who opposed Polk's administration charged that he and other southern Democrats were using the disagreement as an excuse to grab additional land for new slave states.

As he followed events in newspapers from Indianapolis and elsewhere, Wallace eagerly wondered what might happen if the two countries could not reach an agreement on their problems. "I was hungry for war," Wallace admitted. "Had I not been reading about it all my life?" Despite the excitement, he resolved to take an exam before the state supreme court to enable him to win his license as an attorney.

News of fighting between American and Mexican forces, however, caused Wallace to neglect his law studies. "What I really knew had become gelatinous pulp in the cells of my brain," he said. Worse was to come. When he finally presented himself at the statehouse for the exam, he saw that one of the examining judges was Isaac Blackford, who had been the victim of a prank played on him years before by Wallace and a friend. Struggling to finish the exam, Wallace turned in his answers with a note to Blackford reading: "I hope the foregoing answers will be to your satisfaction more than they are to mine; whether they are or not, I shall go to Mexico." A few days later, Wallace received a reply from Blackford saying the court had "no objection to your going to Mexico."

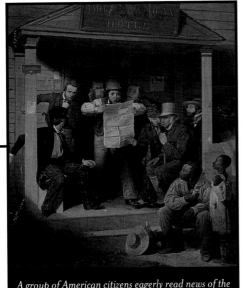

A group of American citizens eagerly read news of the conflict with Mexico during the 1840s.

LIBRARY OF CONGRESS

When Congress declared war on Mexico on May 13, 1846, the country prepared itself for the conflict. The federal government called upon Indiana to provide enough troops for three regiments. Eager to join the fight, Wallace rented a room on Washington Street and turned it into a recruiting office, complete with an American flag and a flyer reading "FOR MEXICO. FALL IN." Within three days, he had recruited enough men for a company and received appointment as its second lieutenant at a monthly salary of twenty-five dollars.

Thousands of Indianapolis residents gathered to see the soldiers off. One of those who watched as Wallace prepared to leave by wagon for Edinburgh and then by railroad to a camp on the Ohio River was his father, David, who would die in 1859. The elder Wallace took his son's hand and said: "Good-bye. Come back a man." The farewell reduced the nineteen-year-old rookie soldier to tears.

Camped on the northern shore of the Ohio River between Jeffersonville and New Albany, Wallace's company received its supplies and was assigned to the First Indiana Infantry Regiment. On July 5, as a fife and drum corps played "Yankee Doodle," the regiment marched onboard a steamboat that would take them down the Mississippi River to New Orleans. From there, a clipper ship took them across the Gulf of Mexico to the war in Mexico. "Now, indeed, I was a soldier," said Wallace. "My name was on the roster and the national uniform on my back."

In late July the First Indiana arrived at its new home, Los Brazos de Santiago, located near the mouth of the Rio Grande River. On the morning of his arrival, Wallace took a look at the sandy, bare area and did not like what he saw. "No town, no grass, not a tree," he said. The regiment soon received orders to take over a camp located ten miles up from the mouth of the Rio Grande. "I remember yet," Wallace said years later, "the sense of desolateness that shocked me viewing the place for the first time."

For the next several months, the Hoosier troops remained at their shabby camp, far away from the fighting being conducted by General Zachary Taylor, known by the soldiers under him as "Old Rough and Ready" for his simple uniform and grubby appearance. Sudden storms from the Gulf of Mexico blew down the regiment's tents and soaked whatever they owned. They had no clean drinking water; the nearby river offered water composed of part sand and yellow mud. For food, they had only beans, pickled pork, shrimp taken from the river, and biscuits filled with brown bugs. The biscuits were hard enough that some men used pieces of them as flints for their muskets.

The bad food and unsafe water combined to make many of the men ill with diarrhea. Many were also stricken with measles and other diseases. So many men died, Wallace noted, that there was not enough time in the day to bury them with the proper military honors. Funerals had to be held at night as well. Soon they ran out of lumber to make coffins. Instead, the dead were buried wrapped in blankets. The wind blew so hard at times that those who had been buried in the sands were uncovered. "Truly we live in the midst of death," Wallace wrote to his brother William.

Trying to keep them occupied, the regiment's commanding officer ordered the men to conduct drills. As one of the youngest officers, Wallace had the unpleasant task of leading the drills, the soldiers sweating in their woolen uniforms in the hot afternoon sun. This did not make him popular with his troops.

Wallace won the respect of the regiment, however, by displaying courage before one of his men, Private Perry Stipp, who had once threatened to kill Wallace in revenge for the tough drilling. Leaving the camp one day to hunt for food with a party of other soldiers, including Stipp, Wallace saw what appeared to be a group of Mexican bandits. Joined by a nervous Stipp, Wallace quietly crept up on the party, only to discover they were members of his own regiment out hunting as they were. From then on, Stipp, impressed by Wallace's courage, became one of his fiercest defenders among the Hoosier soldiers.

In December, the First Indiana finally received orders from General Robert Patterson to move from its barren camp on the river to Walnut Springs near Monterey where General Taylor had his headquarters. After a long trip by boat and foot, the tired regiment neared its destination. The men were just six miles from Walnut Springs when they received new orders from General Taylor

Lew Wallace as he appeared while serving as a young officer during the Mexican War.

31

MS. LEW WALLACE COLLECTION, INSHS

to "return to the accursed camp at the mouth of the Rio Grande," Wallace remembered.

The change in orders so angered the regiment's commanding officer, Lieutenant Colonel Christian Nave, that he resigned on the spot. During its long march back to where it had started, the regiment received further direction from Taylor that a portion of the men were to return to their original camp, while others were assigned to take command of the important town of Matamoros in northern Mexico. "This put us all in better spirits," said Wallace, one of the lucky ones to be ordered to Matamoros.

Years later, during the Civil War, Wallace learned from General Patterson that he had felt so sorry for the First Indiana that he had ordered them to Walnut Springs without Taylor's knowledge. Patterson told Wallace he had "never seen men in the service in such a state of neglect and suffering."

During the slow voyage to Matamoros on the steamboat *Enterprise*, the regiment ran low on rations. Five men were sent to hunt for whatever food they could find. Mexican guerrillas from a nearby town ambushed the party, killing three and mutilating the bodies. Volunteers, including Wallace, who led Company H, stormed off the boat and attacked the town. In their first combat, the American troops drove the enemy forces from the town, suffering one killed and four wounded in the process. Wallace watched as the First Indiana buried its dead on the banks of the river. "Poor boys!" he said. "They had their mourners at home, if not there."

It would not be the last time Wallace witnessed the results of combat. The Indiana troops were in Matamoros until February 1847, when they were ordered back to Walnut Springs. The Hoosiers were left behind again, however, when Taylor clashed with Mexican forces led by General Antonio López de Santa Anna. Wallace, armed with a shotgun, received permission to ride with a captain from the Third Indiana Infantry to the front lines. Halfway to their destination, the men stopped for food and rest at a house occupied by a small number of soldiers from Kentucky.

While munching on crackers and onions, Wallace and his companion learned that the house had been surrounded by Mexican troops. During the night, Wallace lay on the roof and fired at the enemy with his shotgun. For three days the Americans were surrounded. By the time the Mexicans left, Wallace had missed the major fighting. Taylor and his outnumbered troops defeated the Mexicans at the Battle of Buena Vista. The decisive victory made Taylor a hero in the United States.

Finally reaching Buena Vista, Wallace toured what remained of the battlefield with soldiers

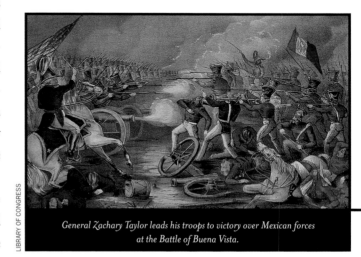

LIBRARY OF CONGRESS

General Zachary Taylor leads his troops to victory over Mexican forces at the Battle of Buena Vista.

33

who had been involved in the fighting. He saw large amounts of abanonded equipment and numerous dead men and horses scattered across the ground. "The earth and rocks were in places black with blood," he said. Soldiers were digging trenches in which to bury the dead and others were "hauling the unfortunate in and depositing them in ghastly rows by the pits."

The scenes Wallace witnessed at Buena Vista were horrible. What angered him, however, was not the cruelty of war but rather a charge passed from Jefferson Davis, who commanded a regiment from Mississippi, to Taylor that troops from the Second Indiana Infantry had been cowards during the battle. Wallace, who believed the charge cruel and unjust, argued for years on behalf of the Hoosier soldiers. He believed so deeply in the soldiers' innocence that he campaigned against Taylor when the general ran successfully as a member of the Whig Party for president in 1848. Wallace, who had been a Whig like his father, ran a weekly newspaper opposed to Taylor.

On May 24, 1847, Wallace and the First Indiana were ordered back to the United States. While waiting at the mouth of the Rio Grande River for ships to take them home, the regiment discovered that the bones of the dead men they had buried at the old camp had been exposed by the winds. One of Wallace's last duties during the war was to rebury his former comrades.

Despite the horrors he had seen, Wallace had no regrets about the year he spent as a soldier or the "righteousness of the war." With his duty to his country done, Wallace considered what he wanted to do with his life once he reached home. As he traveled onboard a steamboat up the Mississippi River, Wallace decided he would use the $280 he had saved and stored in his trunk to finance six months of studying Latin and mathematics at a university. Unfortunately, a fellow officer, a person Wallace had considered a friend, stole his money. Luckily, Wallace had enough cash left to make it back to Indianapolis.

After a week of rest, Wallace returned to his father's office and resumed studying law in hopes of obtaining the license that he had failed to gain before leaving for the war. He also resumed work on his book about the conquest of Mexico by the Spanish. "The writing had been a habit, and a good one, and I resolved to stick to it," Wallace said. As time passed, he worked on the novel whenever he had spare time. Wallace discovered that he could stop writing in the middle of a sentence and still "weeks later, whether on the street or in an assemblage, I could begin where the stop occurred and go on exactly as if the manuscript were before me."

Now twenty-one years old, Wallace was described by a female friend, Mary Clemmer, as a handsome man with black hair, black eyes, and a fine, bushy mustache. "In a crowd anywhere you would single him out as a king of men," said Clemmer. For some time, Wallace had been thinking about marriage. During a visit to Crawfordsville in 1848, he attended a party given by the wife of Henry S. Lane, his former commander during the Mexican War. At the Lanes' home, Wallace met and became fascinated with Susan Arnold Elston, the daughter of a rich local businessman, Major Isaac C. Elston. "She was beautiful in my eyes when I first saw her,"

Daguerreotypes of Lew and Susan Wallace, circa 1850s.

said Wallace, who set out to convince her to marry him. He had competition, however, including an older successful lawyer, a rich man, a businessman, and a preacher.

Success followed success for Wallace in the next year. In the spring of 1849 Susan accepted his marriage proposal; they were wed three years later. That fall, he successfully passed his exams before the state supreme court and received his license as an attorney. In addition to the license, Wallace received a note from his old opponent Judge Blackford reading: "Permit me to congratulate you upon your safe return from Mexico." Embarrassed about how he had treated the judge in the past, Wallace went to Blackford to apologize. The judge laughed and accepted the apology, and the two men became lifelong friends.

Realizing there were already too many lawyers in Indianapolis, and those that remembered his youthful jokes would never "admit the possibility of his knowing more than they," Wallace decided to open a practice in the town of his childhood, Covington. The village also had the advantage of being only thirty or so miles from Crawfordsville, the hometown of his fiancée Susan.

Wallace's office in Covington had only a few pieces of furniture—a table, stove, and a number of law books. Finishing the furnishings was his violin, which he played for relaxation while the rest of the town slept. Wallace continued to rely on his violin for comfort and inspiration the rest of his life.

When he opened his office, Wallace had only a dollar and seventy-five cents in his pocket. That day he learned that the bank that issued the dollar had failed, making the paper money worthless. At first, Wallace attracted only a few clients. He received a helping hand from Judge Joseph Ristine, who hired him to record entries for the Fountain County clerk's office. Wallace earned enough from this job to buy a new set of clothes. To repay Ristine for his kindness, the young lawyer aided him in his campaign as a delegate to Indiana's 1850 constitutional convention.

In addition to helping Ristine, Wallace's work on the judge's behalf led to winning recognition for himself. William Mallory, Ristine's opponent in the election, argued that Ristine, as county clerk, was not eligible to be elected as a convention delegate. Wallace wrote an anonymous article in a local newspaper denouncing Mallory. Guessing the author's identity, Mallory answered the article with one filled with harsh words about Wallace's character.

As Wallace later noted in his autobiography, those living in

Fountain County in those days were "primitive in habits, large-hearted, Western in spirit." Instead of settling their difficulties in court, they would rather have used their fists. During a political meeting in a town called Chambersburg, Mallory and Wallace both spoke to the crowd. During Wallace's speech, Mallory approached him and laid a hand on his arm. "This was justification enough," said Wallace, "and I struck him."

Writing his brother about the fight, Wallace noted the two men "went at it amidst indescribable noise and confusion. I buried my fingers deep in his guzzle, turned his head sideways, and hit him five good ones on the jaw." Found guilty of assault and battery, Wallace had to pay a fine. He did finish his speech and spoke so well that the crowd passed the hat and raised money to pay his fine. From that point on, Wallace had plenty of business for his law practice.

During his time in Covington, Wallace became friends with two of Indiana's leading figures. They were Edward A. Hannegan, a former Democratic U.S. senator and diplomat, and Daniel W. Voorhees, a fellow lawyer and future senator who often stopped by Wallace's office to have his friend play popular songs of the day on his fiddle.

One fine day, Voorhees and Wallace traveled to Danville, Illinois, to attend the court meeting there. That night, they stopped at a tavern in Danville and found standing at the fireplace three of the Hoosier State's best storytellers—Hannegan, Dan Mace, and John Petit. Standing near them were two lawyers from Illinois whom Wallace did not know.

The men began to swap stories and jokes with one another. The talk went on until midnight. Wallace became fascinated with one of the men from Illinois. The man in question was tall and plainly dressed with a long nose, large mouth, hollow cheeks, large hands, and slender arms. Wallace noted that the gentleman from

Illinois kept crossing and uncrossing his legs as he told his stories. "Altogether I thought him the gauntest, quaintest, and most positively ugly man who had ever attracted me enough for study," Wallace said. Whenever the man talked, however, Wallace could not help but be captivated by his storytelling abilities.

By the end of the evening, the other men had exhausted their stories and the Illinois lawyer, Abraham Lincoln, held the floor without opposition. If someone had told Wallace that one day Lincoln would be president and savior of the country, Wallace said he would have laughed at the idea. "Afterwards," he said, "I came to know him better and then I did not laugh." Indeed, Lincoln would play a large role in Wallace's life in the troubled years to come for the United States.

Chapter 4

Defending *the* Union

The 1850s proved to be a happy period in Lew Wallace's life. He obtained success both professionally and personally. In 1850 he won the Democratic party's nomination for prosecuting attorney for Indiana's First Congressional District and won election to the office. To help him win cases (guilty verdicts in the state supreme court earned him ten dollars), he had witnesses sign for the testimony they had given to the grand jury. If a witness gave a different account when the case reached court, Wallace would produce his signed statement and warn him about the "pains of perjury."

Wallace worked hard as prosecuting attorney and achieved financial success. On May 6, 1852, he and Susan Arnold Elston

Wallace holds his young son Henry Lane Wallace in this daguerreotype from the 1850s.

40

FROM THE COLLECTIONS OF THE GENERAL LEW WALLACE STUDY AND MUSEUM, CRAWFORDSVILLE, INDIANA

were married. The couple had a number of interests in common, including books and music. While Lew played the violin, his wife accompanied him on her guitar. She wrote poetry good enough to be published in newspapers and magazines. Later in life, Susan published fascinating accounts of her travels to far-off lands with her husband. "What of success has come to me," Wallace once said, "all that I am, in fact, is owing to her."

On February 17, 1853, Lew and Susan's only child, a son, Henry Lane Wallace, was born. He was named after Lew's former commanding officer and brother-in-law. The family moved to Crawfordsville in April 1853, and Wallace established a law practice in his new hometown. Susan's father gave the couple land next to his home, and they lived in a small, one-story cottage on the property.

Wallace completed a draft of his novel on the conquest of Mexico in 1853 and "laid it away with downright regret." He had no plans for publishing the book. On one occasion, he had read a few chapters of the book to Dr. Charles White, president of Wabash College in Crawfordsville. According to Susan, White "listened politely, took off his spectacles, and then gravely advised Mr. Wallace to abandon the field of authorship." (White died long before the book's publication in 1873.)

A second disappointment occurred when Wallace received a visit from an agent supposedly representing Charles Scribner's Sons, a leading publishing house. The agent read Wallace's manuscript and told him he would be happy to recommend it for publication. All he needed was fifteen dollars as payment for the time he spent reviewing the manuscript. Wallace paid the man the fee, and the agent left town.

"By-and-by," said Wallace, "not hearing from Scribners, I awoke to the fact of having entertained a confidence man; still I could not help laughing." The man's "modest" request had completely fooled Wallace. He wondered if there had been others in Crawfordsville taken in by the trick, as the city had "always been notoriously literary."

Although unlucky as an author, Wallace found success in Hoosier politics. At the age of twenty-nine, he received the Democratic Party's nomination for state senator from Montgomery County and won the election over his Republican opponent by just one hundred votes in the 1856 election.

Taking his seat in the Indiana senate, where he received three dollars for each day in session, Wallace introduced two pieces of legislation. Both went down to defeat. One would have tightened Indiana's lax divorce law that made it quite easy for those wishing to end a marriage to do so. The other bill changed the method by which U.S. senators were elected. Instead of having senators picked by the state legislature, the bill written by Wallace would have let voters decide whom to send to Washington, D.C. (The direct election of senators by voters finally came to be in 1913.)

The reform measures championed by Wallace paled in comparison to the single great issue of the day—slavery. Debate about slavery had turned violent in the 1850s. The Kansas-Nebraska Act passed by the U.S. Congress in 1854 had given settlers in Kansas and Nebraska the right to vote on whether or not slavery should be allowed in those territories.

In 1856 Kansas became the scene of bloody fighting between antislavery and proslavery settlers battling to see who could control the territory. Those who opposed slavery in the North were also shocked by the U.S. Supreme Court's decision in the Dred Scott case. The Court ruled that Congress did not have the power to stop the spread of slavery into western territories as slaves had no rights under the U.S. Constitution.

Wallace opposed the institution of slavery and believed southern leaders were "arrogant, selfish and inconsiderate of the feelings as

LATEST FROM CHARLESTON

SUMTER ON FIRE!!

REBELS FIRING ON THE BURNING FORT!!

Northern citizens are stunned by the news of the South Carolina militia firing on federal forces at Fort Sumter in this illustration from Harper's Pictorial History of the Great Rebellion.

well as interests of the . . . North." Still, he believed northern abolitionists who sought to end slavery everywhere were "fanatics and wild men" who failed to see that their efforts might tear the country apart. He expected the abolitionists would be the ones to "strike the first blow" and start a war between the North and South. He resolved to join whatever side promised to save the Union.

Believing that war might break out at any moment, Wallace prepared himself to be ready to offer his services. He had never cast aside his "love of military life" and began to read whatever books he could on the subject. In the spring of 1856 he also organized a military company in Crawfordsville, recruiting sixty-five men to join a group that came to be known as the Montgomery Guards. The state provided the company with arms and equipment, but they had to provide their own tents, uniforms, and band.

After reading a magazine article about the colorful uniforms and fearless fighting maneuvers used by the Zouaves, a French unit from Algeria in North Africa, Wallace outfitted and trained the Montgomery Guards in the Zouave system. Through Wallace's disciplined leadership and hard work, the Guards won a reputation as one of the finest military organizations in the Hoosier State.

Although cheered by many in their home-town, the Guards were looked down on by the city's "solid citizens," who viewed the preparation for a possible war as foolish and a waste of time and money. Wallace told his men that their hard work would be rewarded one day. He was proved right. The majority of the Guards who served in the Civil War did so as officers,

IHS, KC160

Wallace carried this image of his wife with him in a locket throughout his service in the Civil War.

ranging in rank from lieutenant all the way up to major general.

The election of Republican Abraham Lincoln as president in 1860 brought the crisis between the North and South to a head. Democratic leaders in the southern states had loudly declared they would never agree to be governed by a man who had previously sought an end to slavery's expansion westward and who had called the institution evil. Months before Lincoln's inauguration as president, Wallace attended a meeting of Indiana Democrats at the Palmer House hotel in Indianapolis to discuss what to do if the southern states seceded from the Union.

IHS, ENGLISH COLLECTION, C7048

Oliver P. Morton, the Republican who served as governor of the Hoosier State during the Civil War.

Some of the speakers at the meeting claimed that Democrats in Indiana had no choice if war were to happen—they should support the South. Shocked at what he heard, Wallace left the meeting. One of the Democratic leaders, a judge, saw Wallace leave and stopped him outside the hotel to urge him to return and support the South, as they would need a man with his military experience if there would be fighting. "This is my native state," Wallace told the judge. "I will not leave it to serve the South. Down the street yonder is the old cemetery where my father lies there going to dust. If I fight, I tell you, it shall be for his bones."

Wallace crossed the street to call on Indiana Governor Oliver P. Morton. At one time, Morton had been a student of Professor Samuel K. Hoshour with Wallace and a fellow Democrat. Morton, however, had left the Democratic party and joined the Republicans, and Wallace had spoken harshly against him for doing so. Now, he went to Morton, apologized for his previous actions, and told him about the meeting. He also offered his services to the governor if the South went ahead with its threat to secede from the Union. Morton took Wallace's hand and told him he would be the first man he called if war came.

Late on the afternoon of Saturday, April 13, Wallace got up to speak before a jury at the Clinton County Circuit Court in Frankfort when a telegraph operator burst into the room. He told the judge he had a telegram for Wallace. The message from Morton said: "Sumter has been fired on. Come immediately." Wallace left the case to his law partner to finish and jumped on a horse for the ten-mile ride to the nearest railroad station, where he took a train to Indianapolis to "become a soldier of the Union."

The next morning, Wallace met with Morton at the statehouse and accepted his offer to become the state's adjutant general and help to fill its quota of six regiments called for by President Lincoln. In addition to accepting Morton's offer, Wallace received a promise from the governor that he could command one of the regiments. By Monday, Wallace had started work on his job. Messages poured in from every part of the state about the formation of military companies to meet the crisis.

The state fairgrounds on the near north side of the city became a camp for the new volunteers. The site became known as Camp Morton. Wallace made arrangements so that when officers and their men arrived at Indianapolis's central railroad station they were greeted by either a brass band or a fife and drum corps. As crowds cheered, the volunteers were then marched to Camp Morton, where they were given food and drink and could find a roof under which to sleep.

Thomas Wise Durham, a student and farmer from Waveland, Indiana, remembered being sworn into service by Wallace. Durham

PATRIOTS YOUR COUNTRY NEEDS YOU!

THE UNION FOREVER!

Wanted--25 Men

To fill the ranks of the "INDIANA SNAKE KILLERS," in Colonel Scribner's Regiment at Camp Noble, New Albany. Enquire of *A.B. Naylor or W. Harvey Jr Alton --*

Camp Noble, Aug. 30th, 1861.

JOHN SEXTON, Captain,
JOHN CURRY, 1st Lieutenant,
G. W. WINDELL, 2d Lieut.

A call for men from New Albany, Indiana, to fight for the Union cause in a regiment to be known as the "Indiana Snake Killers."

said Wallace told him and the other men that it would be their "duty to obey orders." Although many in the North believed the war would be over quickly, Wallace warned the new recruits that it would "not be over in three months or a year, but will be a long and bloody conflict," Durham remembered.

By midnight Friday Wallace reported to Morton that Indiana had raised more than double the number of troops required by the president. With his duty done, Wallace asked Morton for the chance to command a regiment of his own. Although the governor had hoped Wallace might stay on in the job as adjutant general, he agreed to Wallace's request and placed him in charge of the Eleventh Indiana Volunteer Infantry as its colonel.

Wallace quickly assumed command of the regiment, which numbered about a thousand men. He had already bought a thousand Zouave uniforms and rented an old freight depot to use as barracks for his new troops.

Wallace drilled his men in the Zouave system. Instead of having orders shouted by officers, men were told what to do by the blowing of bugles. The regiment did its marching "on the run or double-quick," Wallace noted. The soldiers also crouched or crawled on their bellies to fire at the enemy. By the time the regiment received orders to leave Indianapolis for Evansville, it had received praise for its discipline from local newspapers and fame nationwide thanks to Wallace's stirring call for the regiment to take as its rallying cry "Remember Buena Vista!"

Soldiers from the Eleventh Indiana storm across a covered bridge over the Potomoc River to attack Confederate forces at Romney, Virginia. The victory made Wallace a hero early in the war.

The regiment first went to Evansville in southern Indiana to stop and search boats on the Ohio River to make sure they were not carrying supplies to Confederate forces. In early June 1861, the Eleventh Indiana received orders to travel east to Cumberland, Maryland, to help Union forces there under the command of General Robert Patterson. Once in Maryland, the regiment guarded an important part of the Baltimore and Ohio Railroad. Learning of a rebel force in the nearby town of Romney, Virginia, Wallace decided to "take the initiative" and attack the enemy. He took about five hundred men, marched them all night through the mountains, and arrived

Wallace and his Eleventh Indiana staff on service for the Union army in western Virginia.

IHS, C5200

in Romney at dawn the next morning. The Confederates had about twice the number of men as did the Hoosier regiment, but after a brief fight the rebels fled from the town.

Although only a small skirmish in the war, Wallace's "splendid dash on Romney," as President Lincoln called the battle, came at a time when citizens in the North were anxious to hear news of any success by the Union army. Artists from both *Frank Leslie's Illustrated Weekly* and *Harper's Weekly* published drawings of Wallace and his staff. A reporter from Leslie's noted that Wallace "is loved by his officers . . . and by his men to a point of devotion; and it is little to say that they would follow wherever he led, no matter what lay before them." Wallace appreciated the attention, saying it was all "very sweet, indeed." He particularly valued a note of congratulations from Winfield Scott, general in chief of the Union army.

After its original ninety-day enlistment expired, the Eleventh Indiana and its commander returned to Indiana in July 1861. There, Wallace reorganized the regiment with men who had pledged to serve the Union cause for the next three years.

Wallace's next chance for action, honor, and glory came in February 1862, during a Union campaign against crucial Confederate forts located in north-central Tennessee. For the attack, the Union soldiers were led by a general from Galena, Illinois, named Ulysses S. Grant. A graduate of West Point and a veteran of the Mexican War, Grant planned to seize Fort Henry on the Tennessee River and Fort Donelson on the Cumberland River.

By this time, Wallace had received promotion to brigadier general for his distinguished service in Maryland. Wallace had to watch as Union gunboats pounded Fort Henry with shells and forced its surrender on February 6. As Grant prepared to move next against Fort Donelson, Wallace was disappointed to be left behind to guard Fort Henry.

On February 14 Wallace received orders from Grant to bring his troops to join the attack on Fort Donelson. Meeting with Grant at his headquarters, Wallace was put in charge of the Third Division numbering approximately six thousand men. Grant told him to take a position in the center of the line for the upcoming battle and make sure the enemy did not escape. General John McClernand's division was on the right of the line, and General C. F. Smith's division was on the left.

Leaving Grant's headquarters, Wallace thought to himself, "Now—now, certainly, I will see a great battle." He was right. The first victory went to the rebel forces at the fort, as they drove off with their fire Union gunboats attacking from the river. Encouraged by their success, Confederate commanders decided to have their troops attempt to smash through Grant's forces the next day and flee to Nashville, Tennessee. That day and during the night the Union troops had to endure frigid temperatures, snow, and shelling from the fort. "We walked about and beat our bodies to keep up circulation," Wallace remembered, "teeth chattering meanwhile like castanets."

Early in the morning on February 15, Grant had left his headquarters to consult with Andrew Foote, who commanded the Union gunboats. "When I left the National line to visit Flag-Officer Foote," Grant said in his memoirs, "I had no idea that there would be any engagement on land unless I brought it myself." He was proved wrong. Rebel soldiers broke out of their fort and pounced on McClernand's division.

Wallace heard the sounds of the battle, which swelled in volume until it "bore likeness to a distant train of empty cars rushing over a creaking bridge." At about eight o'clock, a messenger from McClernand informed Wallace that soldiers in his division were running low on ammunition and needed immediate help. At first, Wallace declined to send reinforcements, as Grant had ordered him not to take "aggressive" action. After receiving a second plea for help from McClernand, however, Wallace sent a portion of his division to help stop the Confederate assault.

Riding to the action on his horse, John (also called "Old

A drummer boy in the Zouave uniform of the Eleventh Indiana during its attack on Fort Donelson.

IHS, LEW WALLACE COLLECTION, M292

Balley" by Hoosier soldiers), Wallace saw Union troops fleeing from the battle and heard the shouts and yells from the advancing Confederates. One officer rode by on his horse shouting: "We are cut to pieces."

Acting quickly and without orders, Wallace moved the rest of his division to be ready to meet the rebels, successfully repelling three attacks and helping to steady the Union line. The next day, an aide to Grant sent Wallace a note reading: "I speak advisedly. God bless you! You did save the day on the right!"

Seizing advantage of the situation, Grant ordered a counterattack by McClernand and Smith. With his forces still battered from the morning's action, McClernand asked Wallace to make the attack. On the left, Smith and his troops

Union troops during their successful campaign against Confederate soldiers manning the defenses at Fort Donelson.

LIBRARY OF CONGRESS

moved against Fort Donelson. Smith led the way by putting his cap on the tip of his sword, holding the sword aloft, and calling out: "No flinching now, my lads. Here—this is the way!" Strengthened with the addition of his old regiment, the Eleventh Indiana, Wallace moved against Fort Donelson on the right, telling his men, "You have been wanting a fight—you have got it. Hell's before you."

Thomas Wise Durham, who participated in the battle with the Eleventh Indiana, said the regiment attacked the rebels using Zouave tactics. As they advanced, the men dropped to the ground and crawled toward the enemy, letting the Confederates fire over their heads. The men in the Eleventh Indiana then sprang to their feet and gave "them a volley and at them with bayonet." Wallace's men won back the ground lost during the day and by nightfall had command of a hill overlooking the fort.

On February 16 Grant received a note from the Confederate commander, General Simon Bolivar Buckner, a fellow West Point graduate and friend of Grant's who had lent him money when Grant left the army in 1854. Buckner asked for a meeting to discuss terms to end the fighting.

In a reply that made him famous throughout the North, Grant responded: "No terms except unconditional and immediate surrender can be accepted. I propose to move immediately on your works." Although Buckner thought Grant's note "ungenerous and unchivalrous," he agreed with the terms and had the Confederates lay down their arms. The Union had won a major victory.

Although Grant gave most of the credit for the triumph to Smith, his old teacher at West Point, Wallace received his share of glory. The citizens of Crawfordsville sent him a beautiful sword in honor of his victory at Fort Donelson. In March 1862, at thirty-four years of age, Wallace received promotion to major general, the highest rank then possible. He became the youngest person to hold that rank in the Union army.

Wallace yearned for further action. "I find my interest in battles rather increased than otherwise—in fact, I like the excitement, and in very truth," he wrote his wife, Susan, "I never heard music as fascinating and grand as that of battle." He soon had a chance to hear that "music" again at the Battle of Shiloh. This time, however, Wallace would not enjoy the tune.

Union General Henry Halleck, Wallace's relentless enemy during the war.

Chapter 5

Shiloh *and* Monocacy

With the spectacular Union victory at Fort Donelson, the road seemed clear for General Ulysses S. Grant and his approximately forty thousand-man force to move against the Confederates. Union officers hoped to seize Corinth, Mississippi, an important railroad junction.

Grant's success, however, had raised the envy of his superior, Henry Halleck, nicknamed Old Brains by his fellow officers. Halleck complained to officials in Washington, D.C., that Grant had failed to communicate his movements to him. There were also rumors that Grant had been drinking, which had been a problem for him earlier in his career. Halleck removed Grant from command

and replaced him with General C. F. Smith.

By March 1862, however, Grant had been placed back in charge and had concentrated his forces along the Tennessee River. Grant placed his headquarters at Savannah, Tennessee, about nine miles downstream from where his troops were stationed at Pittsburg Landing, a docking place for steamboats traveling along the Tennessee River.

At Savannah, Grant waited for the arrival of General Don Carlos Buell and his twenty-five thousand soldiers. What Grant and the Union army did not know was that Confederate General Albert Sidney Johnston had gathered a force of approximately forty thousand men at Corinth and planned on attacking Grant before Buell could join him. "I would fight them if they were a million," Johnston confidently said.

One man did expect that something was stirring in the Confederate camp: Lew Wallace. He commanded the Third Division, which numbered about six thousand men. The division included many veterans of the fight at Fort Donelson. The soldiers were proud to be part of "Lew Wallace's fighting crowd."

The Third Division had been stationed at Crump's Landing, about five to six miles away from the main Union army at Pittsburg Landing. Separated from the

IHS, BASS PHOTO COMPANY COLLECTION, P130

General Ulysses S. Grant, surprised at Shiloh by Confederate forces, later blamed his near defeat on Wallace's supposed tardiness in responding to his orders. After the war, Grant would soften his attitude about Wallace's efforts at the battle.

main army, Wallace worried he might be attacked by Confederate troops coming from Purdy, Tennessee. He had had his men make improvements to the Shunpike Road that connected his forces with the right of the Union line, held by the First Division led by General William Tecumseh Sherman. Sherman's force had located itself near a small Methodist log meetinghouse called Shiloh, a Biblical name meaning "a place of peace."

As the sun set on April 4, Wallace received a report from one of his scouts, Horace Bell, that Johnston's Confederate army had begun to move from Corinth. Wallace sent a message to Grant at Savannah telling him of the news, but it never reached its destination.

LIBRARY OF CONGRESS

57

Shocked at first by the Confederate advance on his position at Shiloh, General William Tecumseh Sherman managed to rally his troops to meet the threat.

Although some of his soldiers had clashed with the rebels on April 5, Sherman remained confident that he was in no danger. He became furious with an officer from an Ohio regiment who reported the approach of a large rebel army, telling him he could "take his damn regiment back to Ohio!" Grant even wrote to Halleck that he had "scarcely the faintest idea of an attack being made upon us."

As Sherman's troops rose from their tents and began to prepare their breakfasts early on the morning of Sunday, April 6, they were shocked to see thousands of Confederates advancing on their lines shouting their rebel yell. "My God, we're attacked!" Sherman said, as he saw an aide shot down by his side.

Many of the rookie Union soldiers fled from the fighting, seeking shelter miles behind the lines beneath a bluff on the Tennessee River. Others, however, including forces under General Benjamin Prentiss, a Mexican War veteran, stubbornly held off the advancing enemy.

The fighting at Shiloh was some of the fiercest of the war. Union reinforcements who rushed to help their comrades were greeted by one terrified soldier who yelled at them: "For God's sake don't go out there, you will all be killed." Sherman, who worked hard all day to rally his men and had a number of horses shot out from under him, wrote his wife after the battle that "the scenes on the field would have cured anybody of war."

The center of the Union line, which became known as the Hornet's Nest, saw Prentiss and his men battling to live up to Grant's orders to hold their position "at all hazards." Prentiss and the survivors of his division finally surrendered late in the day after holding off the Confederates for almost six hours. Another intense struggle erupted at a nearby peach orchard. Rebel commander Johnston led a charge there that finally routed Union troops.

Returning to the Confederate lines, however, Johnston received a wound to his leg, cutting an artery. He bled to death. The South had lost a valiant officer and perhaps its final chance for success at Shiloh.

At Crump's Landing, Wallace had been awakened early that morning by a sentry who reported he heard gunfire coming from up the river. Wallace gave orders to have his division ready to march wherever they were needed. He concentrated the bulk of his forces at Stoney Lonesome, just up the road from Crump's Landing. Accompanied by Whitelaw Reid, a reporter from the *Cincinnati Gazette* who had been a guest in his tent, Wallace rode with his officers to the river to await orders onboard a steamboat. At about 8:30 a.m., Grant, traveling on the gunboat *Tigress*, pulled up alongside to discuss what to do.

Grant ordered Wallace to hold his division in readiness "to march in any direction" and then left to check on the situation at Pittsburg Landing. As Grant's boat disappeared around a bend in the river, Wallace turned to his officers and said: "Gentlemen, we will get our horses and do our waiting at Stoney Lonesome." He left behind a horse tied to an elm tree so any messenger from Grant could use it to report to him. For the next several hours, as the sounds of gunfire echoed in the distance, Wallace waited impatiently for orders from Grant. He even sent his aide, Captain Ross, back to Crump's Landing to serve as a guide.

At about 11:30 a.m., Captain Ross and another rider, Captain A. S. Baxter, Grant's chief quartermaster, appeared. Baxter presented Wallace with an unsigned order that read: "You will leave sufficient force at Crump's Landing to guard the public property there; with the rest of the division march and form junction with the right of the army. Form line of battle at right angle with the river, and be governed by circumstances." Baxter told Wallace that Grant gave him the order verbally and he had put the order in writing himself. He also noted that the Union forces were successfully driving back the Confederates.

An engraving of Wallace in his Union army uniform.

INDIANA STATE LIBRARY

Union and Confederate armies face one another during the Battle of Shiloh.

Unfortunately for Wallace, one of his officers placed the written order from Baxter under his sword belt, forgot he had put it there, and lost it during the battle. Wallace allowed his men to eat a quick lunch and had them on the march for the battlefield at noon.

Not knowing that Sherman's men had already been pushed back from their original position by the Confederate charge, Wallace pondered what road to take to reach the right of the army. Taking the River Road, which had been flooded, meant a march of eight and three-quarter miles—six miles to Pittsburg Landing and another two and three-quarter miles to reach Sherman's camp. "So, to save the two and three-quarter miles," said Wallace, "and because it was nearer the right and in better condition, I decided to go by the Shunpike [Road]."

Grant, however, believed his instructions to Wallace were to move his troops to Pittsburg Landing via the River Road. "But my order was verbal," Grant admitted in his memoirs, "and to a staff officer who was to deliver it to General Wallace, so that I am not competent to say just what order the General actually received." Grant learned years later that Wallace had been using the Shunpike Road as the expected avenue for reinforcements from the Second Division led by W. H. L. Wallace (no relation to Lew Wallace).

Unaware of the Union army's disastrous position, Wallace received the shock of his life when Captain Rowley of Grant's staff rode up to hurry his division along at about 2:00 p.m. Only then did Wallace discover that Sherman had been driven back from his camp and the entire Union army was in danger of being driven into the Tennessee River. Wallace realized that he and his men were "actually in the rear of the whole Confederate army!"

Wallace thought for a time about continuing the march and springing on the rebel force from the rear, perhaps surprising them and giving Grant's army time to regroup. Rowley, however, had orders from Grant for Wallace to lead his men directly to Pittsburg Landing as quickly as possible.

Instead of having his men simply turn around for the march back to Pittsburg Landing, Wallace countermarched his division, bringing those at the rear of the column forward. He did so because he believed he might have to battle his way through the enemy to reach Grant. Wallace wanted those "regiments whose fighting qualities commanded my confidence to the front." The wet and muddy road conditions further slowed the division's march to the battle.

As his tired men finally neared their destination, Wallace saw stragglers from the battle. The terrified men called out: "We're cut to pieces! Go back while you can!"

Wallace's Third Division arrived on the battlefield at about 6:30 p.m., too late in the day to help. The Union army had been

A series of photographs showing the scene of the Battle of Shiloh years later. Pictured are Pittsburg Landing (opposite page, above), "Bloody Pond" (opposite page, below), the Sunken Road (above), and the bridge over Owl Creek (below).

/ WALLACE COLLECTION, M292

pushed back two miles by the Confederate attack. General Pierre Beauregard, who had taken over for Johnston upon his death, sent a message to Jefferson Davis, president of the Confederacy, that the rebel forces had gained "a complete victory, driving the enemy from every position." Beauregard believed he had Grant "just where I wanted him and could finish him up in the morning."

As rain drenched the battlefield and the wounded cried out in the night, however, Grant remained determined to snatch victory from the jaws of defeat. Encountering Grant seeking shelter from the rain under a tree, Sherman noted that they had "had the devil's own day, haven't we?"

"Yes," Grant responded. "Lick 'em tomorrow, though."

Strengthened by the arrival of Wallace's division and reinforcements from General Buell, the Union army counterattacked the enemy on the second day and won back much of the ground it had lost the previous day. During the fighting, Wallace and his men came across a tent used as a bar by Union soldiers that had been labeled "Paradise." Confederates who seized the tent on the first day of the battle had written beneath its name "Lost." Victorious Union troops added the name "Regained" as they swept the enemy from the field.

The triumph came at a tremendous price. Approaching a brook named Shiloh Run, Wallace saw dead men lying so thick that his horse picked his way through them only reluctantly. The smell of death was so strong that Wallace, in trying to escape from it, mistakenly rode through a swamp. Approximately twenty thousand Confederate and Union soldiers were killed and wounded during the two-day battle. This number exceeded by far the losses suffered in all of the previous battles of the war.

Although a victory for the Union, the enormous losses at Shiloh shocked the public. At first, Grant received much of the blame, with reporters claiming he had been completely surprised by the Confederates. Rumors were also spread that Grant had been drinking and he was even removed from control of his army and replaced by Halleck. Over time, however, Grant regained command. President Abraham Lincoln never lost faith in Grant, telling one Pennsylvania politician who called for the general's removal: "I can't spare this man; he fights."

Wallace became a handy scapegoat for the bloodbath at Shiloh. He did not help his cause by complaining about Halleck's performance to a group of officers he met on the army's slow advance to Corinth. Unfortunately for Wallace, these officers happened to be members of Halleck's own staff. Wallace also later criticized Halleck and Grant in testimony before a congressional committee.

As a West Point graduate, Halleck, whom Lincoln appointed as general-in-chief of all Union armies, distrusted officers like Wallace, who initially received their appointments through political connections. "It seems little better than murder to give important command to men as . . . Lew Wallace," Halleck later said, "yet it seems impossible to prevent it."

The men who served under Wallace supported their commander's actions at Shiloh. They blamed regular army officers such as Grant and Halleck for sticking together to make sure that those who served in the army as volunteer officers did not receive the honors due them.

The praise Wallace received for his generalship at Fort Donelson, said Durham of the Eleventh Indiana who served at Shiloh, "made the West Pointers . . . jealous and they were determined to down him." Wallace also had suspicions that those in power were watching him closely, waiting for any chance to halt his rise to greatness. "I am made conscious . . . of being an object of jealousy," he wrote his wife Susan, "and to feel also that my progress is carefully watched by those who, having the power, stand ready to push me the instant I topple."

In late June 1862 Wallace returned to Indiana for two weeks of leave. A week into his rest, he received a telegram from Governor Oliver P. Morton calling for him to come to Indianapolis. When Wallace reported to Morton, the governor asked him to make speeches aimed at drawing more recruits to the Union cause. Instead, Wallace requested to return to his division and resume command. Morton replied: "There is nothing doing there." The governor showed Wallace a telegram from Secretary of War Edwin Stanton ordering the general to report to Morton. Wallace had been removed from command of the Third Division. "I was on the shelf," Wallace said.

Despite this setback, Wallace remained determined to aid the war effort. He helped to repair his tattered reputation by assisting in saving two key Union cities—Cincinnati, Ohio, and Washington, D.C.—from Confederate attack.

On August 30, 1862, the Confederates had won a major triumph at Richmond, Kentucky. The victorious general, Kirby Smith, tried to further his success by sending troops under the command of Henry Heth to possibly capture Cincinnati. The Ohio River community of about two hundred thousand people lay undefended against the oncoming rebels. Wallace received orders to travel to Cincinnati and take command.

Members of Wallace's staff urged him to refuse the order, as there were only a small number of soldiers and few guns available to defend the city. They feared that Wallace's "enemies" were setting him up to fail. Wallace said to "leave the city to the enemy without an effort to save it would be cowardly; beside that, there is a resource you do not see."

The "resource" Wallace spoke of was the city's citizens. When Wallace arrived in Cincinnati on September 1, 1862, he set in motion an ambitious plan to prepare to meet an expected Confederate attack. He established military control of the city, closed all businesses, and called upon every able-bodied man to take up shovels and dig trenches. "Patriotism, duty, honor, self-preservation call them to the labor, and it must be performed equally by all classes," Wallace said in an announcement printed in area newspapers.

Elaborate defenses were soon ready in Cincinnati and the nearby towns of Covington and Newport, Kentucky. As Heth's army approached Cincinnati, volunteer soldiers, called "Squirrel Hunters" by Wallace, flocked to aid in the defense of the area. Wallace let rebel spies penetrate the city's defenses so they could report back to Heth about what might await him if he dared to move against Wallace. On September 12 a messenger galloped into the city to report that the Confederates had gone. The next day the city's regiments paraded through Cincinnati to receive the cheers of their neighbors. Wallace called it "one of the gladdest days of my life."

Although lauded by Cincinnati newspapers and politicians for his role in saving the city from being taken by rebel forces, his effort did not win Wallace a return to action. He did all he could to convince Union officials to get him back into battle, calling on influential Indiana politicians, including his brother-in-law, U.S. Senator Henry S. Lane, to argue his case with President Lincoln. The president, however, also received pressure from Halleck to keep Wallace away from the war.

Lincoln seemed unsure what to do with Wallace. He complained to a visitor: "Halleck wants to kick Wallace out, and Lane wants me to kick Halleck out."

The visitor replied: "Well, I'll tell you how to fix it to the satisfaction of both parties."

"How is that?" asked Lincoln.

"Why," the visitor said, "kick 'em both out."

The "turning-point," as Wallace termed it, in the reestablish-

A famous Alexander Gardner portrait photograph of President Abraham Lincoln. This is one of the rare photographs of Lincoln looking directly at the viewer. It shows a tired president with heavy lines on his face.

ment of his military career occurred on March 12, 1864. On that date he received orders to take command of the Eighth Army Corps and the Middle Department, which was headquartered in Baltimore, Maryland. Wallace's command included the entire state of Delaware and all of Maryland west to the Monocacy River.

"It was President Lincoln's own suggestion—good enough in itself," Wallace remembered about his new assignment. "Then, when I heard that General Halleck had called upon the President, and in person protested against the assignment, there was added sweetness to it."

Shortly after receiving his orders, Wallace traveled to Washington to meet with Lincoln about his new duties. Lincoln, Wallace said, laid his hand upon the general's shoulder and told him, "I believed it right to give you a chance, Wallace." It had been two years since Wallace had last seen the president, and he noticed that the strain of war had taken its toll on Lincoln. "His face was thinner and more worn," said Wallace, "and I thought the stoop he had brought with him from his home in Illinois more decided."

When the meeting ended, the president called Wallace back into the room and noted that he had almost forgotten that there was a vote approaching in Maryland on a new constitution that outlawed slavery in that key border state (a slave state that had not seceded from the Union). "Don't you forget it," Lincoln said of the election.

The election also became the subject of Wallace's subsequent meeting with Secretary of War Stanton. "It is kindness," Stanton said, "saying it [the election] will be your first trial." Stanton told Wallace that the president was in favor of abolition in this state not covered by the Emancipation Proclamation, which had freed slaves in those states no longer a part of the Union. Lincoln, however, did not want it to appear that the election had been rigged by the use of force.

Maryland had been a trouble spot ever since the war started. A large number of Confederate sympathizers lived there. Early in the war, a mob in Baltimore had attacked a Massachusetts regiment on its way through the city.

With the election on a new Maryland constitution set for April 6, 1864, Wallace swung into action. Petitioned by supporters of abolition to send troops to the polls to ensure a safe election, the new commander of the Middle Department met with Maryland governor Augustus Bradford. The two men came up with a plan whereby Wallace would send the petitions for troops to Bradford, who would then make a written request for the soldiers to Wallace. Troops were eventually sent to every doubtful precinct in Maryland and produced the desired results. In many instances, Wallace said, the sight of the blue-coated Union soldiers at the polling place "so enraged the Secessionists they refused to go to the polls."

Wallace's able handling of the election pleased Lincoln, who called the general to Washington for a meeting. The president praised Wallace's handling of this delicate matter, noting he had handled it "beautifully." Stanton agreed with Lincoln's view, noting those who opposed the abolition amendment could not say the federal government "used the bayonet in the election. If the governor did, that's a different thing." Wallace's skills in handling his vital department, however, were soon put to an even sterner test.

In mid-June 1864, while Confederate General Robert E. Lee and Union General Ulysses S. Grant were locked in combat outside of the Confederate capital of Richmond, Virginia, Lee decided upon a daring plan to help his battered army. Lee sent troops under the command of Jubal "Old Jube" Early, a veteran of many battles, into the Shenandoah Valley. Once there, Early would strike at a Union force under General David Hunter, cross the Potomac River, and possibly threaten Washington, D.C.

Early and his men set out on their mission on June 13. The

Confederate raid would, Lee hoped, accomplish two things. One, it might alarm officials in Washington enough so that they would order troops northward to defend the city, weakening Grant's forces enough to give Lee's army a chance to drive them away from Richmond. Or, Lee reasoned, the raid might encourage Grant to strike first, perhaps a costly frontal assault that would reduce his strength enough for the South to regain the offensive.

There seemed to be no belief on Lee's part that Early might enter Washington. "His orders were merely to threaten the city, and when I suggested to him the idea of capturing it he said it would be impossible," Early recalled after the war. Lee was almost proven wrong.

By July 1 Early's soldiers had chased two Union armies—one under Hunter and the other commanded by General Franz Sigel—out of the Shenandoah Valley. The road to Washington was now open. The Union's reaction to the raid was con-fused at best; Grant even telegraphed to Halleck on July 3 that Early's army remained at Richmond.

One person who did suspect what was happening was Wallace. A day before Grant's message to Halleck, Wallace had met with John W. Garrett, president of the Baltimore and Ohio Railroad and a staunch supporter of the Union. Garrett's railroad agents at Cumberland and Harper's Ferry reported

Confederate General Jubal Early and his forces threatened Washington, D.C., in 1864.

the appearance of rebel troops.

Without any orders from Washing-

NORTH WIND PICTURE ARCHIVES

ton, and without at first informing his superiors, Wallace acted. In asking himself what could be the Confederates' objective, Wallace could come up with only one to justify the risks involved—the capture of Washington. On the night of July 4, Wallace and an aide took a train to Monocacy Junction to survey the potential battlefield.

In deciding to make a stand at Monocacy, Wallace ran over in his mind what might happen if the Union capital were to be captured by the Confederates. He noted there were ships being repaired at the navy yard that would be destroyed, millions of dollars of bonds in the treasury department ripe for the taking, and supplies of all sorts ready to be captured and used by the South. Taking the Union capital might also help the Confederates finally win help from such foreign countries as England and France.

One thought in particular hardened Wallace's determination to hold his ground. It was, he said, the thought of President Lincoln running from the back door of the White House "just as some gray-garbed Confederate . . . burst in the front door." Wallace had a force of approximately two thousand "raw and untried" soldiers to meet Early's army. Still, he hoped he might be able to make the commander of the rebel force reveal the size of his force and his intended objective, and if the objective was Washington, delay him enough to give Grant the time to send troops north to protect the city.

Early's and Wallace's forces first met on July 7 just outside of Frederick, Maryland. This initial skirmish went to Wallace, as the Confederates withdrew near nightfall. Wallace sent a message to Halleck noting that the rebels "were handsomely repulsed." Wallace received a further boost that night when five thousand soldiers of the Third Division of the Sixth Corps under General James Ricketts arrived on the scene. The men had been sent north by Grant. By the evening of July 8, however, Wallace pulled his men out of

Frederick and made his stand east of the Monocacy River.

The next morning, July 9, the main body of Early's army, which nearly doubled Wallace's numbers, hurled itself at the federal position. The battle lasted for nearly six hours. Union troops withstood numerous attacks before being forced to retreat toward Baltimore. The Union forces had lost 98 killed, 594 wounded, and 1,188 missing. Early reported losses of

Secretary of War Edwin Stanton. Stanton, an attorney, had served as attorney general in the administration of President James Buchanan.

IHS, LEW WALLACE COLLECTION, M292

anywhere from 600 to 700 men. Wallace sent a message to Halleck that he had been "overwhelmed" by the Confederate numbers and was "retreating with a foot-sore, battered, and half-demoralized column."

Despite the gloomy tone of Wallace's battle report, he and his men had accomplished their task—they had delayed Early's march on Washington by one full day. Early resumed his march on the city on July 10 and reached the outskirts of Washington the next day.

But Early was too late; Grant had sent enough reinforcements to beat back any assault by the rebels. Although Early attempted an attack on July 12, a battle witnessed firsthand by President Lincoln, the rebel general knew he was too late. He retreated, but told an officer on his staff, "Major, we haven't taken Washington, but we've scared Abe Lincoln like hell!"

Famed Civil War photographer Mathew Brady took this portrait of Wallace at his studio on Pennsylvania Avenue in Washington, D.C.

LIBRARY OF CONGRESS

Wallace received little credit at first for helping save Washington. In fact, on July 11 he received orders that he was to give up his command of the Middle Department to General E. O. C. Ord. That same day, an obviously upset Wallace sent a telegram to Secretary of War Stanton reading: "Does Genl. Ord report to me, or am I to understand that he relieves me of command of the Department. If so, what am I to do?"

The tide soon turned on Wallace's behalf as officials began to realize that his daring stand at Monocacy had rescued the capital from capture by the Confederates. In a July 24 letter to a friend, Wallace reported that Stanton had complimented him on the battle, saying "it was timely, well-delivered, well-managed, and saved Washington City." He indicated the stories about his removal from his job were "all 'bosh.' On the contrary, you can set me *down* as on the *rise*." Just four days later Wallace received orders from the War Department, under the direction of President Lincoln, to resume command of the Middle Department and Eighth Army Corps.

Writing his brother William on September 23, 1864, Wallace said he could say "what no other general officer in the army can—that a defeat did more for me than the victories I've been engaged in." The Battle of Monocacy, as it came to be known, saved Washington, "and the authorities acknowledge the service and are grateful for it," Wallace added.

Even Wallace's battlefield foe praised his actions at Monocacy. Years after the battle, Wallace met Confederate General John B. Gordon, then a U.S. senator. During a conversation at a White House reception, Wallace reported Gordon as saying that the general had been "the only person who had whipped him during the war," even though the rebels had won possession of the field. Gordon said Wallace and his men had "snatched Washington out of our hands—there was the defeat."

Even Grant, who had failed to support Wallace's actions at Shiloh, appreciated Wallace's role during the gallant stand at Monocacy. In his best-selling memoirs, published just before his death, Grant noted that if Early had been just one day earlier, he could have taken Washington before the arrival of the reinforcements Grant had sent. "General Wallace contributed on this occasion, by the defeat of the troops under him," said Grant, "a greater benefit to the cause than often falls to the lot of a commander of equal force to render by means of a victory."

A monument, later erected on the Monocacy battlefield, features Wallace's own statement on the fight: "These men died to save the National Capital, and they did save it."

Actor John Wilkes Booth sneaks into the presidential box at Ford's Theatre and assassinates Abraham Lincoln during a performance of Our American Cousin.

THE PICTURE COLLECTION, THE NEW YORK PUBLIC LIBRARY / ASTOR, LENOX AND TILDEN FOUNDATIONS

Chapter 6

After *the* Battle

On Good Friday, April 14, 1865, President Abraham Lincoln and his wife, Mary, attended a performance of the popular play *Our American Cousin* at Ford's Theatre in Washington, D.C. Just five days before, Confederate General Robert E. Lee had surrendered his army to Union General Ulysses S. Grant at Appomattox Courthouse in Virginia. With the war all but over, the president had joined in the joyful mood that had swept the capital upon hearing of Lee's surrender. "I never felt so happy in my life," Lincoln told his wife.

Arriving at the theater after the play had started, Lincoln and his wife settled into the presidential box to enjoy the comedy, which featured famed actress Laura Keene. Major Henry Rathbone and Clara Harris, his fiancée, accompanied the Lincolns that night. (General Grant and his wife had been invited to attend the play, but they declined the offer in order to visit their children.)

As the presidential party watched the action on stage, John Wilkes Booth, a successful actor and strong supporter of the South, slipped unseen into the box where the president sat. Booth placed his derringer pistol against the back of Lincoln's head and fired.

Making his escape, Booth slashed Major Rathbone with a dagger he held in his left hand before leaping to the stage below, breaking his leg in the process. The astonished crowd heard the well-known actor call out the State of Virginia's motto, "Sic semper tyrannis" (Thus always to tyrants). Others heard him say "The South is avenged!"

Six soldiers carried the critically wounded president—the first in the country's history to be assassinated—out of the theater to a nearby boardinghouse. Lincoln never regained consciousness, and at 7:22 a.m. the next morning, surrounded by doctors and members of the government, he died at the age of fifty-six.

Twelve days after the assassination, Union troops finally found and surrounded Booth, who had taken refuge in a Virginia barn. The soldiers set the barn on fire to force the killer out. One of the soldiers shot Booth as he crept toward the door armed with a carbine. Before he died, Booth said: "Tell my mother—tell my mother that I did it for my country—that I die for my country." As those nearby helped raise his hands so he could see them, Booth uttered his final words: "Useless. Useless."

Booth had not acted alone in killing the president. He had gathered around him a band of followers who planned at first to kidnap Lincoln and hold him in exchange for the release of Confederate prisoners of war. When that plot failed, the new plan called for Booth to murder the president, Lewis Powell (also known

IHS, DANIEL R. WEINBERG LINCOLN CONSPIRATORS COLLECTION, P409

A "Wanted" poster issued by the War Department offering rewards for the capture of presidential assassin Booth and his accomplices, David Herold and John Surratt. The poster incorporated carte-de-visite photographs of the conspirators, including one of Booth that had been produced as a publicity shot for the actor. Both Herold's and Surratt's names are misspelled on the poster.

Portrait of John Wilkes Booth. This is the image that Eugene J. Conger, chief detective in the hunt for Booth, used to identify him as he lay dying on the ground outside the Garrett farm barn.

Members of the military court that tried the Lincoln conspirators. Left to right: David R. Clendenin, C. H. Tompkins, T. M. Harris, Albion P. Howe, James A. Ekin, Lew Wallace, David Hunter, August V. Kautz, Robert S. Foster, John A. Bingham, Henry L. Burnett, and Joseph Holt.

LIBRARY OF CONGRESS

as Lewis Payne) to kill Secretary of State William Seward, and George Atzerodt to assassinate Vice President Andrew Johnson. Although Atzerodt failed to follow through with his assignment, Powell did stab Seward as he lay in bed at his home recovering from a carriage accident. Seward survived Powell's vicious attack, during which several members of the household were injured.

As a shocked nation attempted to deal with the dreadful news coming from Washington, Lew Wallace was on his way back to his post in Baltimore, Maryland, following a mission to Mexico on behalf of Lincoln and Grant.

The government of Mexico under President Benito Juárez had been pushed out of power by troops sent by French ruler Louis Napoléon III, who had placed Austrian archduke Ferdinand Maximilian in charge of the country. Wallace had gone to Mexico to attempt to convince Confederate forces in the region to rejoin the Union, help push the French out of Mexico, and restore Juárez's government to its rightful place. Union officials had also feared that Confederate troops might flee to Mexico and join with the French or establish an independent empire.

Before his death, Lincoln had met with Wallace and approved the mission, but expressed some concern about angering the French. "I suppose it is right," Lincoln told Wallace, "we should help the oppressed." Still, the president had warned the Hoosier general to be careful.

Although Wallace had established contact with General José María Carvajal, one of Juárez's commanders, he had been unable to convince Confederate leaders to agree to the plan. Wallace made it back to Baltimore in time to oversee the display of the casket as part of the president's funeral train journey from Washington to Lincoln's final resting place in Springfield, Illinois.

In early May Wallace received orders to join other Union officers as judges on a military commission authorized by the new president, Andrew Johnson, to try those charged with plotting to kill Lincoln and other government officials. The finding of the commission would be final, with no chance for appeal except directly to President Johnson.

The North wanted vengeance for the dead president. Government officials also wanted quick action. Secretary of the Navy Gideon Welles noted in his diary that Secretary of War Edwin Stanton had told him he wanted those responsible for the assassination "to be tried and executed before President Lincoln was buried."

The eight persons on trial at the Old Arsenal Penitentiary in Washington were Powell, Atzerodt, Samuel Arnold, Edman Spangler, David Herold, Michael O'Laughlin, Dr. Samuel Mudd, and Mary Surratt. Another person involved in the plot, John Surratt, Mary Surratt's son, fled the country.

Mary Surratt, who ran a boardinghouse where the conspirators met, and Dr. Mudd, who treated Booth's broken leg, were charged with aiding those planning the killing. Arnold and O'Laughlin were accused of being involved in the assassination plot. Powell,

Atzerodt, Spangler, and Herold were indicted for their participation in the attacks on government officials. During their confinement, many of the prisoners were shackled and had to wear heavy cloth hoods over their heads.

At first, the military commission met in secret. Only later did the government agree to open the trial to selected members of the public and press. Those who wanted to attend had to receive a special pass from Major General David Hunter, who served as president of the commission. Hundreds of witnesses appeared before the commission on behalf of the prosecution and defense from May 9 to June 29.

During the long, hot days of testimony, Wallace, the only lawyer among the army officers on the commission, passed the time by making sketches of the commission members, the spectators, and all of the defendants except for Mary Surratt, who spent most of the trial with her face hidden by a veil.

Those on trial for the Lincoln assassination had few of the legal rights afforded to defendants today, and some of the evidence presented by the government had been fabricated. Still, the attorneys for those on trial presented a spirited defense that may have won some of the commission to their side. In a June 26 letter to his wife, Wallace wrote that if the commission voted then, "three, if not four, of the eight will be acquitted."

The prosecution, however, continued to hammer away at the accused, even attempting to involve leaders of the Confederacy (especially Jefferson Davis) in the plot. On June 29 the commission met in secret to make its decision. It took the commission only a day and a half to reach a verdict—guilty for all. Powell, Herold, Atzerodt, and Mary Surratt were sentenced to death and were hanged on July 7 at the Old Arsenal Penitentiary.

At the time of the trial, only a few voices were raised in protest in the North. One newspaper, the *New York World*, dismayed by what went on, lashed out at the commission for its "heat and

Sketches of the various conspirators made by Wallace during the trial. Wallace also drew the hoods and ball and chains the accused wore during a portion of the proceedings.

IHS, LEW WALLACE COLLECTION, M292

intolerance." Although debate still rages today on the fairness of the Lincoln conspirators' trial, Wallace never expressed any doubts about the verdict decided by the commission. In 1895 he wrote that the trial "was perfect in every respect. No judicial inquiry was ever more fairly conducted."

Testimony before the commission had included shocking stories of the mistreatment of Union prisoners at the hands of the Confederates. Upon seeing some returned prisoners from a camp on the James River, poet Walt Whitman was moved to ask: "Can

A photograph of the filthy conditions Union prisoners had to endure at Andersonville Prison. The "dead line" can be seen at the right of the photograph, which was taken on August 17, 1864.

those be men? Those little livid brown, ash streaked, monkey-looking dwarfs?—are they not really mummied, dwindled corpses? Probably no more appalling sight was ever seen on this earth." Articles and photographs appeared in northern newspapers describing the horrors of the prisoner of war camps in the South, particularly one in Georgia named Andersonville, commanded by Captain Henry Wirz.

Opened in early 1864, Andersonville had been designed to hold, at most, ten thousand prisoners. By that summer, the camp had three times that number. Men had little or no shelter from the weather, poor food to eat, and filthy water to drink. Weakened by starvation, the prisoners were easy prey for a number of diseases that swept through their ranks. Within the camp, guards established a "dead line." If prisoners dared to touch or cross the line, they would be shot. At one point, 150 prisoners died every day; approximately 13,000 men lost their lives in these dreadful conditions.

Robert Kellogg, a Connecticut soldier and a prisoner of war, remembered the terror he felt at his first sight of Andersonville. The one-time soldiers were now merely "walking skeletons, covered with filth and vermin." Those who were with Kellogg were so shocked by what they saw that they exclaimed: "Can this be hell? God protect us!"

One southern woman who viewed the camp believed the Confederates would "suffer some terrible retribution" for allowing such suffering to happen. "If the Yankees should ever come to southwest Georgia and go to Andersonville and see the graves there," she added, "God have mercy on the land!"

The crowded conditions at Andersonville became worse in part because of the breakdown of the prisoner exchange system used

by the North and South early in the war. When freed slaves and other African Americans joined the Union army to fight for freedom, the Confederate Congress in 1863 approved a policy to return to slavery or to kill captured black soldiers and their officers. Outraged by this decision, the Union government halted the exchange of captured Confederate troops.

In August 1865 Wallace found himself appointed to another commission. This time he

IHS, LEW WALLACE COLLECTION, M292

Wallace made this sketch, eventually titled "Over the Dead Line," during his service on the military commission that tried Confederate Captain Henry Wirz.

served as president of a military court judging Wirz for war crimes involving his treatment of Union prisoners at Andersonville. The trial foreshadowed those held following World War II involving German Nazi officials for their crimes against humanity, including the murder of millions of Jews in what came to be known as the Holocaust.

"The prisoner's defence," Wallace wrote his wife, "will be that he obeyed orders received from his superiors." Wallace went on to say that he expected the investigation to find that Confederate leader Jefferson Davis would be connected with the "criminality" at Andersonville. The commission's work, he added, should take two months—"the hot, unwholesome, malarial months here by the Potomac [River]."

Although the government at first tried to involve Davis, General Lee, and other high-ranking Confederates as accomplices in the horrors at Andersonville, it learned from the mistakes of the Lincoln conspirators' trial and decided to concentrate on Wirz alone.

Wirz is hanged for his crimes as commander of the Andersonville Prison.

LIBRARY OF CONGRESS

Born in Switzerland, Wirz had been a doctor in Louisiana when the Civil War began. He served in the Confederate army as an officer until he received a severe wound to his right arm. Wirz took over as commander of Andersonville in March 1864. Prisoners remembered Wirz as an angry man more worried about preventing them from escaping than easing the horrible conditions at the camp. Upon seeing Wirz during the early days of the trial, Wallace described the Confederate officer as "nervous and fully alarmed, avoids your gaze, and withers and shrivels under the knit brows of the crowd."

Witness after witness testified to the suffering endured by the Union prisoners. "The details of that place of torture are horrible," Wallace wrote his wife. One incident in particular caught Wallace's attention. It involved testimony about a prisoner who, "half dead with thirst," crawled under the dead line to reach a stream for a clean drink of water. The guard on duty shot the man, and the cup he held dropped from his hand and landed beyond the dead line. Wallace produced a sketch he called "Over the Dead Line" and showed it to the other officers on the commission.

Wirz argued that he had just been following orders and should not be punished for doing so, and testimony disagreed on whether or not he had actually ever personally killed a prisoner. Nevertheless, the commission found Wirz guilty and sentenced him to death. President Johnson upheld the decision and, on November 10, the government hanged Wirz on the same ground where the Lincoln conspirators had been executed. Those dedicated to the Confederate cause treated Wirz as a martyred hero. Those who survived Andersonville's terrible conditions, however, recalled a tyrant who did nothing to help their sufferings.

During his duty on both the Lincoln and Wirz commissions, Wallace had continued to be fascinated by the struggles of the republican Mexican government to free itself from the French occupation. He did whatever he could for the Mexican cause, including organizing volunteers from America to fight against the French and raising money and selling bonds in order to help buy arms and equipment for Juárez. "Mexico is uppermost in Lew's mind at present—when he dies, Mexico will be found written on his heart," Susan said in a letter to her mother.

After sending in his resignation from the American army in early November 1865, Wallace worked hard to support the Mexican cause, receiving a commission as a major general in the Mexican army and forming an aid society to inform the American public about what was happening in Mexico. With the help of another Hoosier, Herman Sturm, Wallace managed to send via ship almost two million dollars worth of guns and ammunition to Mexico.

Unfortunately for Wallace, this shipment became caught up in a revolt among Carvajal's soldiers. Wallace was even thrown in jail for a time. Although he called the matter "disgraceful," Wallace did find some humor in the situation, noting that not a shot had been fired nor a person hurt during the revolt. "Whatever the stories may be," he said, "taken altogether, that was the funniest affair I ever beheld." In September 1866 part of the supplies finally reached Mexican forces.

Wallace traveled extensively in Mexico, attempting to contact Juárez's government, seeing again the land he had visited as a young Indiana soldier during the Mexican War, and touring gold mines. By the end of 1866, the French, hounded and pursued by Juárez's forces, began to leave Mexico. Abandoned by the French, Maximilian fought on, only to be captured and executed in the summer of 1867.

Victory for the Mexican cause, however, did not mean triumph for Wallace. He had been promised $100,000 from Carvajal for his work, but the Mexican government refused to honor the agreement. Not until 1882 did the Mexican government finally acknowledge Wallace's ser-

IHS, LEW WALLACE COLLECTION, M292

Fellow Hoosier Herman Sturm aided Wallace in his efforts to supply the Mexican government with arms and ammunition in its battle to oust French forces from its territory.

vices to its country, agreeing to pay him $15,000.

The money, however, remained secondary to Wallace's desire to be remembered for his fight to free Mexico from foreign domination. "Some day," he later wrote to his son, "I may even get some credit for having helped crush out the empire Louis Napoléon tried to plant on our continent."

At the age of forty, Wallace found himself back in Crawfordsville, Indiana, where he resumed his work as a lawyer— a job he had grown to hate. "I never loved the profession. It was a drag," he later admitted. "I worried at it, and it worried me. The routine was simply abominable—horrible."

Mexican General José María Carvajal.

IHS, LEW WALLACE COLLECTION, M292

Politics seemed to offer the chance to regain the excitement Wallace desired. In 1868 he ran for Congress in the Republican primary election against the incumbent, Godlove S. Orth. Wallace lost the primary to Orth. Two years later, Orth announced he would not run again, and Wallace received the Republican nomination for Congress. The Democrats attacked Wallace during the election for his adventure in Mexico, and he lost by approximately four hundred votes.

Frustrated by this setback, Wallace returned to an activity he had enjoyed for years—writing. Inspired by his travels through Mexico, Wallace completed the novel he had started back in 1843 about the fall of Montezuma's Aztec Empire to Spain, *The Fair God.* His service in the Civil War also aided Wallace in writing the warfare scenes in the book. "The experience there gained was invaluable to me," he later told a reporter, "in fact, I don't think I could have got on without it."

In 1873 the Boston publishing firm of Osgood and Company agreed to publish Wallace's manuscript. Samuel R. Crocker, who read and recommended that the book be released to the public, called it "remarkable in theme and treatment." He noted that it read as if it had been translated "from some old Spanish author" who had personally known the true-life people written about in the book.

Although American literary tastes had turned to novels with more down-to-earth themes, the book received high praise from some, especially from critics in England. One reader there called *The Fair God* the "best historical novel that ever was written." The book sold seven thousand copies in its first year and continued to sell well in subsequent years as Wallace's fame as an author grew.

His experience in the Civil War enabled Wallace to accurately capture in his book the sights and sounds of battle. The most thrilling scenes in *The Fair God* are the struggles between the Aztec warriors and Hernando Cortés's Spanish troops. Wallace also used an incident from his life for a description of the priest Mualox, who mystically sees through the eyes of a child the coming of the Spanish conquerors. While living in Covington, Wallace had become friends with a tailor who believed he could hypnotize people. The tailor managed to hypnotize one of his apprentices and had Wallace imagine traveling to a place he knew. Still hypnotized, the boy accurately described the route Wallace had been thinking about.

Achieving his dream of becoming an author caused Wallace some trouble back home in Indiana. "The publication of my first novel was almost enough to ruin my law practice," Wallace remembered. Lawyers opposing him in court cases never failed to mention his work as a novelist, which drew great peals of laughter from the farmers and merchants sitting on juries. "I might as well have appeared in court dressed as a circus clown," Wallace later told Booth Tarkington, another famous Indiana author. Novels, after all, were seen as things to be enjoyed only by women, not by rugged men. Most ministers also preached against reading novels, calling such material sinful.

The ridicule he received from some Hoosiers failed to stop Wallace from starting work on another writing project. In December 1873 he went to the Library of Congress in Washington, D.C., to begin research on what he hoped would be an illustrated magazine article about the three Wise Men and their trip to witness the birth of Jesus Christ. At the time he began to work on his article, Wallace was not influenced by any religious feeling. "I had no convictions about God or Christ," he said. "I neither believed nor disbelieved in them."

At the Library of Congress, Wallace studied the history and geography of the Middle East at the time of the birth of Jesus Christ. "I had never been to the Holy Land," he later wrote. "In making it the location of my story, it was needful not merely to be familiar with its history and geography, I must be able to paint it, water, land, and sky in actual colors."

Also, because the subject he selected had been explored thoroughly in the past by the world's greatest scholars, Wallace was careful to avoid any mistakes about the customs of the people who lived in the Holy Land—the Egyptians, Romans, Greeks, and Jews. "I had to fix every date, certify every surrounding, and deal with things divine as well as human," he noted.

After completing the article, Wallace set it aside in a desk drawer, waiting for "courage" to send it on to a publisher. The story might still be there except for a chance meeting with a fellow veteran of the Civil War.

In September 1876 Wallace traveled by train from Crawfordsville to Indianapolis to attend a soldiers' reunion. As he moved slowly down the aisle of the train, Wallace heard a knock coming from inside a compartment and someone calling his name. When Wallace answered the call, the door opened and he saw Colonel Robert G. Ingersoll, a fellow veteran of Shiloh. Ingersoll had won fame as a powerful political speaker and believer in science and reason. He had also earned ridicule for his spirited questions about God and religion.

Wallace sat beside Ingersoll and agreed to talk with him if he could select the subject. Wallace then asked Ingersoll to consider the questions of whether or not there were a God, a Devil, a Heaven, and a Hell. Wallace said he sat "spellbound" as Ingersoll proceeded to discuss his views on religion with great style and wit. "He surpassed himself," Wallace said of Ingersoll's remarks, "and that is saying a great deal."

After arriving in Indianapolis, Wallace began the long walk to his brother's home northeast of town. Ingersoll had made him "ashamed" of his ignorance about religious matters and he resolved to study the subject. "And while casting round how to set about the study to the best advantage, I thought of the manuscript in my desk," said Wallace. He decided to write on the life of Christ from his birth to his eventual crucifixion.

But what to do about the years between Christ's arrival on earth and his death? "The Christian world would not tolerate a novel with Jesus Christ its hero, and I knew it," said Wallace. Still, the author realized he must always keep Christ in his reader's thoughts as the reader advanced through the book. Wallace decided to tell the story of Christ through the eyes of Judah Ben-Hur, a Jewish noble whose life comes into conflict with his one-time friend Messala, a Roman official in the Holy Land who betrays his friend. Throughout the book Ben-Hur is tied into Christ's life, as well as undergoing thrilling adventures and great tragedies of his own.

IHS, JAY SMALL POSTCARD COLLECTION, P391

The home of Lew and Susan Wallace in Crawfordsville, Indiana.

Wallace worked on his new novel whenever and wherever he could. Occupied with his law profession and other matters during the day, he spent nights at his new home in Crawfordsville, built on land once belonging to Susan's father. On summer days, Wallace would leave his house, take shelter from the sun under the shade of a beech tree, and work on his book. "Its spreading branches," Wallace noted of the tree, "droop to the ground, weighed down by their wealth of foliage, and under them I am shut in as by the walls of a towering green tent."

As page after page of his new book appeared, Wallace examined his writing with a very critical eye. He told a reporter that if a paragraph or chapter was not to his liking, he would throw it away and start again. "It is better to destroy unsatisfactory [work] than to try and patch it up here and there," he said. Wallace also depended upon Susan, never finishing a chapter until he had read it to his wife for her opinion. "In many instances I had great help that way," Wallace noted.

Another crisis for the country, however, kept Wallace away from his new novel. The presidential election of 1876, America's

Lew Wallace writes on a lap desk under the shade of trees on the grounds of his home in Crawfordsville.

94

one hundredth anniversary as a nation, had Democrat Samuel Tilden of New York running against Republican Rutherford B. Hayes of Ohio. When the votes were counted, it seemed as if Tilden had defeated Hayes by approximately 250,000 in the popular vote. Tilden, however, had won only 184 electoral votes, one short of winning the presidency. The electoral votes for the states of Florida, South Carolina, and Louisiana, plus one in Oregon, were up for grabs. For Hayes to be successful, he had to win all of the undecided electoral votes.

Following the Civil War, federal troops had remained in the South to help support the rights of the freed slaves. African Americans had loyally supported the political party—the Republicans—that had worked to free them from bondage and kept soldiers available to make sure they had the chance to vote. Democrats in the South did everything they could to keep black voters away from the polls. President Ulysses S. Grant, a Republican, sent additional troops to the South to keep order. Grant also called upon "visiting statesmen"—men known for their honesty—from both parties to travel South to help ensure a fair count of the disputed votes.

Wallace had the honor of being one of the "statesmen" sent to oversee the counting of votes in Louisiana and Florida. Writing to his wife from Tallahassee, Florida, on November 26, 1876, Wallace expressed his frustration with the attempts by both Democrats and Republicans to win by whatever means necessary. "It is terrible to see the extent to which all classes go in their determination to win," he wrote. "Conscience offers no restraint. Nothing is so common as the resort to perjury, unless it is violence—in short, I do not know whom to believe." Still, Wallace worked hard to support the Republican claim to the disputed electoral votes.

Both the Republicans and Democrats believed that their candidate had won the disputed states. To end the deadlock, the U.S. Congress in January 1877 established an Electoral Commission to rule on the election. By an eight to seven vote, the commission, which voted along party lines, gave all of the disputed electoral votes to Hayes, making him the nineteenth president of the United States.

Behind the scenes, leaders for both parties had worked out a compromise agreement whereby Democrats would withdraw any opposition to Hayes's election if he agreed to withdraw the remaining federal troops from the South, appoint a southerner as part of his Cabinet, and offer increased aid to the region.

With a new Republican administration in office, it seemed as if Wallace might be rewarded for his support of the party during the election. In August 1878 he received a message from Secretary of State William M. Evarts offering him the diplomatic position of minister resident and consul general (the United States did not create the title of ambassador until years later) to Bolivia at a salary of $5,000. Wallace turned down the offer. He wrote President Hayes that he could not go so far away with his family for such a small salary. "The sum would not enable me fairly to represent our country," he said, "and leave me a compensation for two years of life lost."

Just a few weeks later, Wallace turned aside thoughts of monetary reward for a chance to see the West. He accepted an appointment from Hayes as the new governor of the New Mexico Territory for just $2,600 a year. "I accepted because I had traveled in Mexico and had a desire to see the country to which I am going," Wallace told a reporter. He could also now quit his law practice and dream again of a land where Spanish conquistadors once roamed. Wallace did not know it at the time, but his new job would also bring him face to face with an individual who became one of the West's most famous outlaws—William H. Bonney, better known as Billy the Kid.

Chapter 7

The Wild West

At nine o'clock in the evening of September 29, 1878, a horse-drawn carriage clattered to a stop in front of the La Fonda hotel in Santa Fe, the capital city of the New Mexico Territory. Lew Wallace, the territory's new governor, stepped off the carriage and surveyed the narrow streets and the nearby mountains that loomed over the city. He had just endured a long and difficult journey by train and carriage from his home in Crawfordsville, Indiana, to his new post in the southwestern United States.

Wallace was "thankful beyond expression" that his trip over rough roads in a carriage with weak springs that jolted and bucked its occupants at every turn of its wheels had finally ended. "A deadlier instrument of torture was never used in the days of Torquemada [during the Spanish Inquisition]," he wrote to his wife, "without a stop except to change horses—trot, trot, jolt, jolt, bang, bang, incessantly—no rest, no sleep, and cold to the marrow despite two heavy blankets." There were, however, much rougher times ahead for the new governor.

The United States had seized New Mexico at the start of its war with Mexico in 1846. The land had first been settled hundreds of years before by Spanish colonists who established a capital at Santa Fe and built the El Palacio del Gobernador, the Palace of Governors, a block-long building in the center of the city, as the seat of government. It was here where Wallace went the morning after his arrival to inform Samuel B. Axtell, a former San Francisco lawyer and congressman, that he was being replaced as governor.

Axtell had lost his job as a result of his association with a group of politicians and businessmen known as the Santa Fe Ring, which controlled much of the trade that went on in the territory. New Mexico, however, attracted numerous settlers looking for an opportunity to make their fortune. Violence erupted as groups schemed for power. The most serious trouble came in Lincoln County, a huge region (larger than the state of Indiana) of almost thirty thousand miles located in southeastern New Mexico. The trouble there became known as the Lincoln County War.

For many years, Lawrence G. Murphy and his associates, James J. Dolan and John H. Riley, had dominated business in Lincoln County. The monopoly they enjoyed became known as The House. They controlled government supply contracts for Fort Stanton and the Apache Indian agency in the county and used their power to frighten anyone who tried to oppose them.

Competition soon came from such figures as cattleman John S. Chisum, and especially from a partnership formed between attorney Alexander A. McSween and British rancher John S.

Tunstall. The competing groups soon turned to hiring outlaws to fight for their side, including a young William H. Bonney, who became notorious as Billy the Kid.

Born in New York City in 1859, Bonney and his widowed mother had made their way to New Mexico in the 1870s, where she married William H. Antrim. After his mother's death in 1874, Billy scratched out a living as a cowboy and also earned a reputation for his skill with guns. In August 1877 he killed his first man, a blacksmith with whom he had gotten into an argument. Arrested for murder, Billy escaped his captors and became a wanted man. In the fall of 1877 he had made his way to Lincoln County, where at first he worked on behalf of Dolan. Later, he found work at the Tunstall ranch and became friendly with the Englishman.

Lew Wallace at age fifty at about the time he served as governor of the New Mexico Territory.

IHS, LEW WALLACE COLLECTION, M292

99

The tension between the competing groups in Lincoln County reached a fever pitch on February 18, 1878, when a posse led by Lincoln County Sheriff William Brady, a friend of the Murphy-Dolan faction, shot and killed Tunstall on the way back to his ranch. A distraught Billy the Kid is supposed to have vowed after Tunstall's death: "I'll get some of them before I die." McSween organized his own band of desperadoes to fight back. His men, who included Billy, killed Sheriff Brady during an ambush in Lincoln, the county seat.

The two sides battled back and forth for much of July. The

Illustration showing the Palace of Governors and the room in which Wallace wrote the final portions of his best-selling novel Ben-Hur.

SANTA FE

IHS.

GOVERNORS PALACE.

The "BEN-HUR" Room

McSween gang suffered a severe setback when U.S. army troops from Fort Stanton joined with the new sheriff, supported by Murphy, to surround McSween and his followers, who took refuge in the McSween home. To break the stalemate, those surrounding the house set it on fire. Some in the house, including Billy, were able to escape the flames. McSween also tried to escape, but was gunned down.

Alarmed by the violence and rumors that Governor Axtell's administration had been filled with "corruption, fraud, mismanagement, plots and murder," federal officials had turned to Wallace to bring peace to the region. "When I reached Santa Fe," Wallace noted later, "I found that law was practically a nullity, and had no way of asserting itself." After officially informing Axtell about his removal as governor, Wallace turned his attention to restoring law and order in Lincoln County. He received reports from government and military officials indicating that the situation was so bad in Lincoln County no courts could operate safely there.

These alarming accounts caused Wallace to ask President Rutherford B. Hayes to place Lincoln County under martial law and appoint a military commission to try those accused of crimes. Hayes refused Wallace's request, but did issue a proclamation on October 7 calling for the citizens of the county to "disperse and retire peaceably to their respective homes on or before noon of the 13th day of October." Additional troops were also sent to Fort Stanton to assist in maintaining order. These steps seemed to work so well that Wallace, on November 13, issued a proclamation in English and Spanish offering a general pardon for those who had been involved in crimes in the county.

Although most welcomed Wallace's actions, some in the military, especially Lieutenant Colonel Nathan Dudley, believed the proclamation had unfairly accused them of wrongdoing. McSween's wife had also hired a lawyer, Huston Chapman, who charged that Dudley had been responsible for McSween's death and demanded an investigation by the governor.

The contending sides in Lincoln County had finally arranged an end to their conflict, but it did not last long. During a drunken celebration in Lincoln on the evening of February 18, 1879, members of the Dolan faction happened upon Chapman. Harsh words were exchanged and gunfire erupted in the night, hitting Chapman. "My God, I am killed," cried Chapman, as he fell to the ground dead. Billy the Kid witnessed the killing.

The new outbreak of violence finally persuaded Wallace that he needed to travel to Lincoln County and sort matters out personally. Accompanied by General Edward Hatch, commander of the military district of New Mexico, Wallace left Santa Fe on March 1 for the four-day journey on rough roads to his destination.

Upon his arrival in Lincoln, Wallace established his headquarters at a neutral location and set about restoring order. He organized a public meeting at the courthouse to seek evidence on any crimes, sought to have Dudley removed from his command, and ordered the arrest of those responsible for Chapman's killing. In addition, Wallace organized a militia company called the Lincoln County Mounted Rifles (Wallace's critics called them the "Governor's Heelflies") to seek out and bring wanted criminals to justice. One of the wanted men was Billy the Kid. Wallace offered a $1,000 reward for his arrest.

A week after issuing the reward for Billy's arrest, Wallace received a letter from the outlaw. Billy indicated that he had seen the men who had murdered Chapman and offered to testify if the charges against him were dropped. "If it was so that I could appear at Court I could give the desired information," Billy wrote, "but I have indictments against me for things that happened in the last Lincoln County War and am afraid to give up because my enemies would kill me."

An excited Wallace immediately sent Billy a reply, offering to meet with the nineteen-year-old outlaw in secret at nine in the evening the next Monday at the home of John B. Wilson, the justice of the peace and a Tunstall supporter known by Billy. "I have the authority to exempt you from prosecution," Wallace wrote, "if you will testify to what you say you know."

At the appointed hour on the night of March 17, Wallace heard a knock at the door of Wilson's home and told the person to come in. The door opened, and there stood Billy the Kid, a Winchester rifle held in his right hand and a revolver in his left hand. "I was sent for to meet the governor here at 9 o'clock," said Billy. "Is he here?" Wallace rose to his feet, said his name, and shook hands with the bandit.

"Your note gave promise of absolute protection," Billy warily noted.

"Yes," Wallace replied, "and I have been true to my promise."

The governor pointed to Wilson and told Billy that they were the only people in the house. Hearing this, Billy lowered his rifle and placed his revolver in his holster. When the men were seated, Wallace outlined his plan for ensuring Billy's safety if he testified about Chapman's murder at the court's session in two to three weeks. "In return for your doing this," Wallace promised, "I will let you go scot free with a pardon in your pocket for all your misdeeds."

The governor proposed that a "fake" arrest be made so Billy could be placed in jail, safe from any attempts to silence him. "When I finished," Wallace remembered, "the Kid talked over the details of this plan for his fake arrest with a good deal of zest." Billy even suggested that he should be kept in handcuffs during his detention so others would be more willing to believe the arrest had been real. Although Billy did not immediately agree to the governor's proposal, he did promise to write Wallace in a few days

Portrait of famed outlaw "Billy the Kid" Bonney posing with his rifle, circa 1880.

GETTY IMAGES

with his final decision.

On March 20 Billy sent a letter to Wallace accepting his proposal and offering suggestions on how to proceed with the arrest. He told Wallace to be sure that he had men he could depend on to handle the matter. "I am not afraid to die like a man fighting but I would not like to die like a dog unarmed," Billy wrote. The next day, Sheriff George Kimball arrested Billy without any trouble.

At first, Billy was confined in the town's jail. The filthy conditions at the jail inspired him to write on its door: "William Bonney was incarcerated here first time, December 22nd, 1878; second time, March 21st, 1879, and hope I never will be again."

Billy was later moved to better quarters at the home of Juan Patrón, the owner of a store in Lincoln and captain of the Lincoln County Rifles. There, as Wallace reported to officials back in Washington, D.C., the desperado became an object of affection for the local residents, with a few "minstrels of the village actually serenading the fellow in his prison."

Wallace did not bother to keep Billy under strict confinement and offered him "a good many privileges." The governor even visited the outlaw to learn if rumors of Billy's skill with firearms were true. Billy gave Wallace an exhibition of his marksmanship with both rifle and revolver. Wallace complimented the young man on his shooting and asked him if there was a trick to it. Billy said that when he was a boy he noticed that anyone pointing to an object often used his index finger. He decided to do the same with his shooting. "When I lift my revolver, I ask myself, 'Point with your finger' and unconsciously, it makes the aim certain," Billy told Wallace. "There is no failure. I pull the trigger and the bullet goes true to its mark."

When those guarding Billy expressed concern to Wallace about his meeting with an armed outlaw, the governor noted that he was "the last man in New Mexico Billy wanted to kill," as he was the only person who could offer him a pardon for his crimes.

Billy the Kid kept up his end of the bargain with Wallace. When the grand jury convened on April 14, he testified against the men accused of killing Chapman. Four days later, Wallace returned to Santa Fe, rejoining his wife, who had come to New Mexico from Indiana with their son Henry in February. In May, Wallace, accompanied by Susan, returned to Fort Stanton. He appeared there to testify before a military court called to try Lieutenant Colonel Dudley for his alleged misdeeds in the Lincoln County War.

The uncivilized conditions at the fort and the harsh, dry weather caused Susan to write that perhaps the United States "should have another war with Old Mexico to make her take back New Mexico." She complained that the frequent dust storms made everything gritty to the touch and taste. "Yet I have heard of this as the garden spot of the territory," she said. "Garden! There has been no rain for six months, and what can grow in soil made of fire-clay, alkali, and sand?" Tired of the territory, Susan returned to Indiana in October 1879.

Susan's poor opinion of New Mexico may have been heightened by the continued threats of violence against her husband. She had even heard a rumor that Billy the Kid had bragged to people that he intended "to ride into the plaza at Santa Fe, hitch my horse in front of the palace, and put a bullet through Lew Wallace." Of course, she did not know of the secret agreement between the governor and the outlaw concerning immunity given to Billy in return for his testimony.

In fact, Billy showed some concern for the governor's safety. After finishing his testimony before the Dudley court, Wallace prepared to return to Santa Fe with Susan. Before they left Lincoln County, Susan, in a letter to her sister, noted that Billy the Kid, whom she called "a gentlemanly appearing fellow," shook hands with her husband and suggested he have a guard on watch. "I always have," Wallace replied, "and was never surprised in my life." Three calvarymen rode in front and three behind the Wallaces during the uneventful trip back to Santa Fe.

Although the military court cleared Dudley of any wrongdoing, a defeat for Wallace, conditions in Lincoln County had improved. Wallace's actions won praise from New Mexico newspapers, with one noting that it would "not be strange if . . . the renewed prosperity of this Territory is dated from the administration of Governor Wallace."

Trouble, however, came from a former ally: Billy the Kid. The local district attorney had refused to honor Wallace's pardon for Billy's past criminal activity and had attempted to move the case against the outlaw to another county. Alarmed, Billy easily escaped from prison and returned to his life of crime. A new sheriff, Pat Garrett, took on the task of finding Billy and putting him behind bars. Garrett tracked down the outlaw and his gang and captured Billy, who was put on trial for murder at a Mesilla, New Mexico, courtroom in March 1881.

The court found Billy guilty for the murder of Sheriff Brady and sentenced him to hang. In an interview with a Mesilla newspaper, Billy called on Wallace to pardon him, pointing to the "friendly relations" that existed between the two men. "Think it hard that I should be the only one to suffer the extreme penalties of the law," Billy told the reporter.

Wallace refused to act on Billy's behalf, probably because of the bandit's return to thieving and other crimes after his escape from prison. Returned to Lincoln to be hanged, Billy, with the help of a friend who supplied him with a gun, killed two of his guards and made good his escape. Wallace offered a $500 reward for Billy's capture.

On July 14, 1881, Garrett and two deputies tracked down Billy at the home of Pete Maxwell near Fort Sumner. There, Garrett surprised Billy, shot, and killed him. Billy the Kid passed from young outlaw to legend. His adventures were told again and again in magazine articles, books, television programs, and films.

Billy the Kid's death did not end Wallace's troubles. As the governor tried to end the violence in Lincoln County, he also dealt with a group of Ojo Caliente Apache Indians led by Chief Victorio, whom Wallace called "an enemy not to be despised." The Apaches began a series of raids on unsuspecting settlers beginning in the late summer of 1877. After attacking settlements, the Apaches would seek shelter from U.S. troops by riding across the border into Mexico.

Frustrated by having the problem seemingly ignored by officials in Washington, D.C., Wallace traveled throughout the territory to see what could be done. The residents of one town that had been the victim of a recent Indian attack were shocked to see the governor and his party. "Had we been newly raised from the dead," said Wallace, "they could not have shown greater awe." On the return to Santa Fe, a member of the group accompanying the governor shot and killed an Apache warrior who had been following them. Wallace received the Apache's weapons and shield as souvenirs.

Other difficulties plagued Wallace throughout his days as territorial governor. When he first moved into the Palace of Governors in Santa Fe, he noticed the building's poor condition and even called upon a group of local doctors to inspect the Palace to determine if it was fit to serve "as an abode for a family and for offices." The physicians were alarmed at what they saw, noting they would not stable their horses at the east end of the building, the area where the legislature met. Although Wallace tried to win funding from the federal government to renovate the Palace, such a project did not happen until after he had left the territory. Wallace did, however, manage to save from ruin many of New Mexico's early papers and records.

Despite a busy schedule, Wallace found time to explore the countryside for minerals and complete a project he had begun years earlier—his novel, *Ben-Hur*. Wallace had finished a large portion of his book before starting his duties as governor. Whenever he could, usually at night, Wallace retired to a small room in the Palace with only a single window and a rough, pine table. There, by the light of a lamp, he would work to finish his novel. "The ghosts, if they were about, did not disturb me; yet in the hush of that gloomy harborage I beheld the Crucifixion, and strove to write what I beheld," Wallace remembered.

Writing *Ben-Hur* became "a perfect retreat from the annoyances of daily life as they are spun for me by enemies, and friends who might as well be enemies," Wallace noted. Still, the work was long and hard and the governor looked forward to finishing the book. "When I reach the words 'The End' how beautiful they will look to

Several sketches of life in New Mexico and Mexico made by Wallace during his time as territorial governor.

me!" Wallace wrote his wife. "What a long, long work it has been, a labor of love!" Not only had his writing offered him a break from the cares and concerns of his tiring duties as governor, it also led him to become "a believer in God and Christ."

In March 1880 Wallace completed a final draft of his manuscript, which he wrote in purple ink as a way to honor the Easter season. The next month, he took a leave of absence from his duties as governor and traveled, accompanied by Susan, to New York. There he met with Joseph Henry Harper of the Harper and Brothers publishing firm. When he opened the pages of the 200,000-word document Wallace had given him, Harper said: "This is the most beautiful manuscript that has ever come into this house. A bold experiment to make Christ a hero that has been often tried and always failed."

Released to the public on November 12, 1880, at a cost of $1.50 per copy, *Ben-Hur: A Tale of the Christ* sold poorly at first, with only 2,800 copies purchased during its first seven months. Wallace's romantic historical tale had lost favor with many literary critics during this time period, and they gave the book poor reviews. One critic wrote in a San Francisco newspaper protesting as a friend of Christ that "He has been crucified enough already, without having a Territorial Governor after him."

Wallace's book, however, received an enthusiastic response from average readers across the country and around the world. Readers became fascinated by Ben-Hur's adventures, including his escape from a Roman galley during a sea battle with pirates and his duel with Messala during a breathtaking chariot race. In addition, readers were inspired by Ben-Hur's acceptance of Christ's message of compassion and understanding. Ministers and preachers, who had often looked down on novels as a waste of time and even as sinful, urged members of their congregations to read the book.

General Ulysses S. Grant had not read a novel for ten years when he opened a copy Wallace had sent him. He began reading in the morning and could not put it down, finally finishing the book at noon the next day. An owner of a Lafayette, Indiana, store wrote Wallace in 1886 that he "would rather be the author of Ben-Hur than to be President of the United States." By 1889 Harper and Brothers had sold four hundred thousand copies of Wallace's book, which was translated into numerous languages. In 1913 Sears, Roebuck and Company printed a million copies of *Ben-Hur* to sell at thirty-nine cents each. Today, Wallace's work stands as one of the best-selling novels of all time.

By the time Harper and Brothers published *Ben-Hur*, Wallace had grown tired of the daily grind of being New Mexico's territorial governor. He had become particularly frustrated at his failure to convince a divided legislature to agree to approve a number of reform measures. When the New Mexico lawmakers refused to confirm his selection of Eugene Fisk as attorney general for the territory, Wallace waited until the legislature ended its term and placed Fisk in office. A court later ruled that Wallace did not have the power for such an action.

With the election of a new president, James Garfield, a Republican and Civil War veteran, Wallace decided to resign as governor. On March 9, 1881, Wallace submitted his resignation to Garfield. As the governor prepared to leave office, one newspaper in the territory called him "the only respectable and worthy gentleman who was ever appointed to a Federal Office in New Mexico." Wallace waited anxiously for his replacement to come. He expected that whatever attempts at change his successor attempted would fail as his had done. "Every calculation based on experience elsewhere fails in New Mexico," Wallace wrote Susan.

While waiting to leave New Mexico, Wallace wondered what might come next in his life. In Washington, D.C., the new president pondered naming Wallace as ambassador to Paraguay in South America. But on April 13 Garfield began reading a copy of *Ben-Hur* sent to him by Wallace. Fascinated by the book, he read until two o'clock in the morning. In his journal Garfield said the novel "keeps up in dignity and interest." He continued reading the book and decided to send Wallace as head of the American mission to Turkey's capital Constantinople (today's Istanbul), where, Garfield noted, the author could possibly "draw inspiration from the modern east for future literary work."

Garfield finished *Ben-Hur* on April 19 and sent a letter to Wallace praising him for the work he had done. "The theme was difficult; but you handled it with great delicacy and power," Garfield wrote. "With this beautiful and reverent book," Garfield added, "you have lightened the burden of my daily life and renewed our acquaintance which began at Shiloh." The president offered Wallace the diplomatic post of minister resident to Turkey, which Wallace gladly accepted.

Across the left-hand corner of Wallace's official commission as minister to Turkey, dated May 19, 1881, Garfield wrote his initials and the title of the author's book *Ben-Hur*. After a stop in Crawfordsville, Wallace met with Garfield and Secretary of State James Blaine in Washington, D.C., to discuss his new job. "I expect another book out of you. Your official duties will not be

LIBRARY OF CONGRESS

President James Garfield, who appointed Wallace to serve as U.S. minister to Turkey after reading Ben-Hur. Garfield was shot by an assassin at a Washington, D.C., railroad station on July 2, 1881. He died on September 19.

too onerous to allow you to write it," Garfield told Wallace. In June Wallace and his wife set sail from New York on their journey to another new land. The author of *Ben-Hur* would finally have the opportunity to personally see the Holy Land he had written about so well.

Sultan Abdul Hamid II, the ruler of Turkey during Wallace's duty as U.S. minister to the Middle Eastern country.

Chapter 8

The Sultan *and the* Study

T he first meeting between Lew Wallace, the United States's new minister to Turkey, and that Islamic country's supreme ruler, Sultan Abdul Hamid II, happened at an official reception filled with much pomp and circumstance on a balmy day in September 1881 at the sultan's palace, Dolma-Bagtché. These encounters between the sultan and representatives of foreign governments were usually boring affairs. Every step in the meeting followed a strict protocol and schedule. Wallace, however, had other ideas.

Dressed in the uniform of a major general, complete with a sword, Wallace traveled to the sultan's palace with two other Americans, Samuel S. Cox, a congressman and chairman of the

House Foreign Relations Committee, and Edwin A. Grosvenor, a history professor. When the three men arrived at the palace, Ibrahim Bey, one of the sultan's assistants, led them to a room to wait. There the men smoked cigarettes and drank coffee while they prepared for the arrival of carriages to take them to the sultan's favorite residence, Yildiz Kiosk, located about a mile away. Writing later about the day, Grosvenor noted that it was a custom to have foreign diplomats kept waiting for some time before they were presented to the sultan.

Wallace, however, refused to wait. Calmly, he turned to his interpreter, Mr. Gargiulo, and said: "Please say to his excellency, Ibrahim Bey, that I wish to know why the carriages are not here."

"They are coming. They are coming," said the surprised official.

A moment later, with the carriages still absent, Wallace said, "Please say to his excellency that I do not wish to wait."

"But they are here! They are here!" the Bey cried, leading the Americans to the courtyard where the carriages had been waiting all along.

The court officials and other assistants who attended to the sultan's needs had another, greater shock in store for them when Wallace and Hamid, the ruler and spiritual head of the once-great Ottoman Empire, met for the first time. "Later on we were to remark the deathlike pallor of his face," Grosvenor said of Hamid, "the thinness of his lips, and his air of melancholy, almost dejection." At the meeting, Wallace presented letters from President James Garfield to the sultan. In return, Hamid asked about the president's health (Garfield had been shot by an assassin and would later die).

As the interview drew to an end, Wallace turned to Gargiulo and told him to tell the sultan that "as representative of the American people I desire to take his majesty's hand." Grosvenor noted that Wallace's simple suggestion to shake hands with the sultan caused an uproar, as it was not a custom practiced in Turkey. In addition, to have a foreigner and a Christian touch the Muslim ruler seemed "sacrilegious presumption," Grosvenor said.

As Wallace tried to have his request translated so the sultan could understand, Hamid, who noted the disturbance, asked, "What is it? What does his excellency say?" When Wallace's request had been passed along, the sultan seemed puzzled for a moment before he smiled, stepped forward, and shook Wallace's hand. It marked the first time in history that a sultan had done so with anyone.

As the American trio was ushered into a reception room for more coffee after the interview had ended, Grosvenor noticed that a new relationship had developed with the Turks. Those who served the sultan cast puzzled glances at Wallace, the "strange man from the West, who had overridden tradition, and as an equal had pressed their sovereign's hand," Grosvenor said.

The sultan, too, had been impressed with Wallace. They met a few weeks later to discuss problems associated with American missionaries in the country, who were attempting to convert Muslims to Christianity. Both men were sympathetic about the other's religious beliefs, with the sultan noting that mocking Christ "is as blasphemous to a good Moslem as it is to a good Christian."

Wallace later noted that there was "something heroic and terrible in this religion [Islam], in none other I have known does it run through and color the whole life of the believer." Hamid even asked Wallace for a copy of *Ben-Hur* so he could have it translated into his own language. After the meeting, the sultan told a close aide, "I believe that American is an honest man."

During his four years as minister to Turkey, Wallace enjoyed a close relationship with Hamid. Grosvenor said his fellow American had a "personal influence upon the sultan such as no envoy of any foreign nation had exerted before." The sultan sought Wallace's advice a number of times during his stay in Turkey, meeting with him at all hours of the day and night. Wallace had a simple explanation for why he managed to win the ruler's trust: "I did it by telling him the truth, a thing he did not always hear from those around him."

During the summer of 1882, Wallace tried to help Hamid in a crisis between the Turkish government and Great Britain. For years the sultan had enjoyed considerable influence over the country of Egypt. This had lessened as the British and French, who had built the Suez Canal, took control over much of the Egyptian government. Hamid had used his influence to provoke an uprising against this foreign power with the rallying cry "Egypt for Egyptians." The British had responded by sending warships to the area. The Egyptians who had rebelled then threatened to attack the British ships.

Wallace worked hard to arrange a peaceful settlement to the crisis, meeting with both the British ambassador, Lord Dufferin, and the sultan. Unfortunately, he could not get the two sides to reach an agreement. The British landed an army and took control of the country, including the canal. Despite the setback, Wallace had earned the respect of the governments involved for his tireless efforts. He also received a promotion, becoming envoy extraordinary and minister plenipotentiary, the highest rank then available in the American diplomatic service.

During his stay in Turkey, Wallace found the time to travel to the Holy Land, the

Wallace made this drawing of Hamid wearing the traditional fez in February 1885.

IHS, LEW WALLACE COLLECTION, M292

scene of his famous novel. Joined by his wife and sister-in-law, Wallace traveled to Jerusalem. Once there, they set out on a five-day tour of the area, visiting the land where Judah Ben-Hur was supposed to have lived.

For someone who had never been to the region before, Wallace discovered he had described the land in his book with great accuracy. "At every point of the journey over which I traced his [Ben-Hur's] steps to Jerusalem," said Wallace, "I found the descriptive details true to the existing objects and scenes, and I find no reason for making a single change in the text of the book."

Homesick for his native country, Wallace returned to the United States for a break from his diplomatic duties in June 1884. He later observed to a relative that although he had been privileged to travel and learn about other lands, his own country remained "the best, the freest, the happiest one beneath God's sunshine—worth living for and worth dying for, too, whenever the need arises." Wallace and Susan arrived back in New York in June 1884. In talking with reporters, he had nothing but praise for the sultan, noting there existed "no monarch today actually administering a government in Europe who is his superior."

After returning to his Crawfordsville home, Wallace went on the campaign trail, speaking on behalf of Republican presidential candidate James Blaine in his race for the White House against Democrat Grover Cleveland. Wallace also produced an article on

Wearing a pair of pince-nez glasses, Wallace poses for a New York photographer, circa 1880s.

IHS, LEW WALLACE COLLECTION, M292

Wallace relaxes with a book at home in Crawfordsville.

the capture of Fort Donelson for a series of articles on the Civil War in *Century* magazine.

Also in November, Wallace traveled to New York City to meet with his old commander, General Ulysses S. Grant, at his home on Sixty-sixth Street. Although he had been diagnosed by doctors with cancer of the throat—a disease that eventually killed him—Grant had begun work on his memoirs. The same day Wallace visited, Mark Twain, the great American humorist and writer, had paid a call to the former president to attempt to convince him to let him publish Grant's life story.

As the three famous men talked, Julia Grant, the general's wife, noted there were many women in the country that would love to be in her place so they could tell their children they had been "elbow to elbow between two such great authors as Mark Twain and General Wallace." Never at a loss for words, Twain joked with

Grant: "Don't look so cowed, General. You have written a book, too, and when it is published you can hold up your head and let on to be a person of consequence yourself."

Despite Wallace's hard work on behalf of the Republican cause during the presidential campaign, Democrat Cleveland and his running mate, Thomas Hendricks of Indiana, were victorious. Cleveland's election meant that Wallace, a diehard Republican, would have to resign from his post in Turkey to be replaced by a Democrat. Still, he decided to return to Constantinople to serve out the few months left in his term and receive the $3,000 coming to him as salary. Wallace would have to travel alone, however, as Susan had decided to avoid any possible rough seas by remaining behind in Crawfordsville.

He set sail on November 22, 1884, on the ship *City of Chicago*. During his journey, Wallace stopped in London to buy a dog to present to the sultan as a parting present. After examining a number of different dogs, Wallace selected an English mastiff puppy already impressive in size. The dog, whom Wallace named Victorio in honor of the Apache chief who had given him so much trouble in New Mexico, arrived in Turkey a few days after Wallace's return. He had the dog delivered to the sultan at his palace. According to Wallace, those at the palace took one look at the animal and ran, thinking it was a lion! "At last accounts," Wallace wrote his son Henry, "the Sultan keeps him in his bedroom, and the intimacy between the two is said to be most cordial."

Upon his return to Constantinople, Wallace had an interesting conversation with the sultan about his future. According to Wallace, Hamid began the discussion by saying, "The election did not turn out as we hoped."

"No, your majesty," Wallace replied, "and I am sorry for it."

"Are you to remain with us after the new president comes in?" Hamid asked.

"No, there is a custom which has the force of law requiring me to resign my commission," said Wallace.

"Well," the sultan said, "why not, when you leave the service with your own country, take service with me?"

Being careful not to offend the sultan, Wallace thanked him for the "high compliment" but said he could not afford to accept such an offer. He also turned down the sultan's proposal to make him the Turkish ambassador to France or England. Instead, Wallace said he could not agree to such a job unless it would be to represent Turkish interests in America.

The sultan was so determined to have Wallace remain that he even said he would write President Cleveland to ask him to permit Wallace to remain as his country's representative. Unfortunately, Wallace said he could not remain as minister under Cleveland, as he "would be forever trying to explain why I did so to my party."

Finally, on March 4, 1885, Wallace submitted his official resignation by telegram to officials in Washington, D.C. Writing his wife about his resignation, Wallace expressed great satisfaction in the job he had done on behalf of his country. Looking back on all the activities he had been involved with over the years—war, law, politics, writing, and diplomacy—Wallace said he looked upon *Ben-Hur* "as my best performance, and this mission near the sultan as the next best."

Wallace's final audience with the sultan happened on May 14. During the meeting, Hamid made it clear that he considered Wallace to be more than just another diplomat. "Since I have been on the throne," said the sultan, "no foreigner has come to me officially or in private capacity for whom I have had the friendship I have for you." He asked the American to write him at least once a month.

With Wallace now a private citizen, and no longer an official representative of his government, the sultan presented him with a number of gifts. These included the Imperial Decoration of the

Joined by two fellow veterans of the Civil War, Wallace visits the site of what he called the "old wound," the Battle of Shiloh.

MS, LEW WALLACE COLLECTION, INSCA

Medjidie, First Class; a gold cigarette case with a diamond-lined lid; and an album of photographs of the sultan's palaces and parks. Wallace also asked for and received pictures of the sultan and his family.

With his duties as a diplomat complete, Wallace considered what he next would do with his life. After many years of financial troubles, he was finally free of debt and no longer had to return for support to the practice of law, a job he called the "most detestable of human occupations." Dreaming of the future, Wallace wanted to build a study where he would be able to write. "I want to bury myself in a den of books," he said. "I want to saturate myself with the elements of which they are made, and breathe their atmosphere until I am of it."

It took a number of years, however, for Wallace's dream of a study filled with books to come true. In the meantime, he toured the country lecturing on his experiences in Turkey and continued to be involved with

IHS, LEW WALLACE COLLECTION, M292

Wallace participates in one of his favorite pastimes—fishing on the Kankakee River in Indiana.

politics. For the 1888 presidential election, Wallace merged his interests in writing and politics and produced a well-regarded biography of Benjamin Harrison, the Republican candidate and a fellow Hoosier. Although incumbent President Cleveland received more popular votes than Harrison, the Indiana Republican won the Electoral College and became the twenty-third president of the United States.

With all these activities keeping him busy, Wallace still remembered President James Garfield's request upon his appointment to Turkey that he set his next novel in Constantinople. While in

MS, LEW WALLACE COLLECTION, M292

A view of the Blacherne apartment building Wallace had built at 401 North Meridian Street in Indianapolis. Today, the building overlooks the War Memorial and University Park.

Turkey, Wallace had visited the historical archives there to do research for a book on the fall of Emperor Constantine's Christian Constantinople to the Turks under Moslem leader Mohammed II in 1453. Eventually titled *The Prince of India; or, Why Constantinople Fell*, the book has as its main character the Wandering Jew, who, according to legend, abused Christ on the way to his crucifixion. In punishment for his insult, the Wandering Jew was cursed with eternal life, forced to roam the land without rest.

Wallace began work on his new novel in September 1887 and worked at it in fits and starts over the next few years. "The new book grows but—O, so slowly!" Wallace revealed to Henry Alden, the editor of *Harper's Monthly*. Susan wrote a friend not to expect a new book from her husband for several years as he needed to study a number of historical works, some in languages unfamiliar to him.

The book finally appeared in two volumes in 1893. Although Wallace considered *The Prince of India* to be his best book, and Harper and Brothers sold more than 250,000 copies in the first seven months of its release, the work received an unenthusiastic welcome from most critics. Readers expecting another *Ben-Hur* were also disappointed with the book. One even wrote Wallace that he should have stopped writing after *Ben-Hur*.

Swallowing his disappointment at his book's reception, Wallace continued to plan future writing projects, including poems and plays. He even tinkered in his barn in Crawfordsville with a few inventions, receiving patents for such contraptions as railroad equipment and fishing rods.

An 1893 visit to the World's Columbian Exposition in Chicago inspired Wallace to become involved in architecture, which he called "the greatest of the three Arts." Using profits from the success of *Ben-Hur*, he constructed a modern, seven-story apartment building in Indianapolis called the Blacherne, named for a palace in Constantinople. He kept an apartment for himself and used it whenever business took him to the Hoosier capital.

In addition to the Indianapolis apartment, Wallace set out to finally fulfill his grand dream of constructing what he called "a pleasure-house for my soul," a study near his home and beloved beech trees in Crawfordsville. The study's construction occurred between 1895 and 1898 and cost approximately $30,000. Working under plans drawn up by Wallace himself, architect John G. Thurtle produced what one newspaper called "the most beautiful author's study in the world . . . a dream of oriental beauty and luxury."

The study incorporated a number of different architectural

Several interior and exterior views of the Wallace Study in Crawfordsville.

FROM THE COLLECTION OF THE GENERAL LEW WALLACE STUDY AND MUSEUM, CRAWFORDSVILLE, INDIANA

Wallace entertains his young grandson, Lew Wallace Jr., by playing his favorite instrument, the violin.

styles. Wallace modeled the ground's front gate on the abbey of the church of St. Pierre in France. The study's forty-foot-high tower had arched windows and reflected the look of the Cathedral of Pisa. A copper dome and stained-glass skylight reminded Wallace of the mosques he had visited while U.S. minister to Turkey. A limestone molding, which included carved figures of characters from the author's novels, ran around the tower and study. The face of Judah Ben-Hur stood above the study's entrance. A moat stocked with fish was located on the building's east side. (Wallace later had the moat filled in.)

The study's interior had electric and gas lights and a gas fireplace. White oak bookcases lined three of the four walls and were stuffed with books on history, law, and the military. He also filled the study with mementos from his life, including the arms and shield of an Apache warrior killed by Wallace's bodyguards while he served as governor of New Mexico; a Confederate flag captured during the Battle of Monocacy; and a painting of a Turkish princess given to him by the sultan.

Wallace did not sit idle in his "pleasure-house." Instead, he established a regular schedule for his writing, working from nine in the morning until lunch, then resuming work and completing his efforts at four in the afternoon. To keep fit after a day of writing, he either walked in the nearby countryside or rode a horse. "I write from 1,000 to 1,500 words every day," he told a reporter from the *Cincinnati Tribune*. "Then, every day I carefully go over what I have written the previous day, and generally cut it down to 200 or 300 words or throw it out entirely." Although he refused to tell the reporter the title or character of his next book, Wallace had talked of taking the Wandering Jew from *The Prince of India* and having him sail with Columbus on his voyage to the Americas in 1492.

Instead of a new novel, however, his publishers, Harper and Brothers, suggested he write his autobiography. At the age of seventy, Wallace set out to capture on paper his rich and full life. "I begin to believe in the possibility of making it a readable book," he wrote his publishers in September 1897.

Talking to a reporter from a Texas newspaper about the book, Wallace said he was surprised to discover how well he remembered conversations and incidents from his career. "The most important ones of my life seem to have been photographed on my brain," he said, "and I can have them in their fullest detail."

There were interruptions for Wallace as he attempted to write his memoirs. When America declared war on Spain in 1898, the former Civil War general offered his services once again to his country, offering to raise and lead a force of African American soldiers to fight in the coming battle. No offer for an army commission for Wallace, however, came from the government.

Secure in his fame as the author of *Ben-Hur*, Wallace became an inspiration to a new generation of Hoosier writers, including such well-known novelists as Meredith Nicholson and Booth Tarkington. These two men, along with poet James Whitcomb Riley and humorist George Ade, were the leading figures of what came to be known as the golden age of Indiana literature.

Nicholson, author of the best-selling *The House of a Thousand Candles*, knew Wallace from an early age. His father had been a member of the Montgomery Guards and had served in the Eleventh Indiana Infantry Regiment during the Civil War. Growing up as he did in Crawfordsville, Nicholson said that Wallace had been "the good knight of my childhood, the man who stood to me for heroic and romantic things."

When Wallace returned from Turkey, Nicholson, then eighteen years old, was working as a clerk in the Indianapolis law office of the general's brother, William. One day Wallace visited the offices and Nicholson asked him for his opinion on some of his first poems.

The veteran writer offered kind advice to the young Nicholson.

Years later, Nicholson could still remember the way Wallace looked and talked. Nicholson was particularly taken with the former general's dark eyes and beautiful voice. He compared hearing Wallace talk to the experience of reading a book—"a mighty good book at that."

Nicholson noted one visit Wallace made to his brother's law office where he sat down, tipped his chair back, pulled from his pocket a bag of peanuts, and casually ate them while he talked. Wallace then produced the jeweled cigarette case given to him by the sultan and lit a cigarette as his impressed audience looked on. "He held his head high and there was a great pride in him; but he was the kindliest and gentlest of spirits," Nicholson said.

Tarkington, who considered Wallace to be as close to him as an older brother, was ten years old when he first met the Civil War hero. He and his father were standing in front of a newspaper

Wallace sits on a bench reading a book with his grandsons near the formal pool, located northeast of his study.

office in Indianapolis when they saw Wallace walking down the street. Tarkington's father called Wallace over to meet his son, and the two shook hands. "He frightened me; but there was something reassuring about him too," Tarkington said, "and I felt then . . . a little explosion of pride within me that General Wallace and my father and I were fellow citizens of the United States."

When Tarkington tried and failed to find publishers for his stories in the 1890s, Wallace was there to offer him encouragement. He pointed out to the young writer that even publishing a book did not mean success, pointing to the trouble *The Fair God* had caused him in his law practice. "Remember," Wallace told Tarkington, "a great many of our citizens would rather have a loafer in the family than a writer."

Wallace continued to offer his assistance after Tarkington had achieved some literary success with the publication of two books, *The Gentleman from Indiana* and *Monsieur Beaucaire*. "You have always been kind to 'the little brothers'—especially to the little Hoosier brothers who try to follow in the procession in which you lead," Tarkington wrote Wallace.

The city of Crawfordsville was home to many authors. In addition to Wallace, the community included such writers as Nicholson, Maurice and Will Henry Thompson, and Mary Hannah and Caroline Virginia Krout. The gathering together of such artists

With the help of a cane, Wallace strolls through the grounds surrounding his study in Crawfordsville.

FROM THE LOCAL HISTORY COLLECTIONS OF THE CRAWFORDSVILLE DISTRICT PUBLIC LIBRARY, INDIANA with the pen won for the community the name "The Athens of In-diana," after the ancient Greek city known for its cultured citizens.

Wallace's neighbors in Craw-fordsville remembered him for his kindness, as he was always will-ing to show visitors around his property. He could often be found in long conversations about the Civil War with other veterans of the conflict. Wallace became so wrapped up in these talks that he lost track of time. Susan would have to send a servant to tell him it was time for dinner.

A portrait of Wallace taken a year before his death in 1905.

IHS, LEW WALLACE COLLECTION, M292

Ill health plagued Wallace during the last few years of his life. He could walk only with the help of a cane and became so weak he had to stop work on his autobiography. He had completed writing up to the retreat at the Battle of Monocacy. Nearly a lifetime of smoking had caught up with Wallace. Stomach cancer robbed his body of its ability to absorb nourishment from food. Relatives, including his grand-children, gathered around him at his Crawfordsville home.

At the end, only his doctors, nurses, his wife, son, and daugh-ter-in-law were at his side. According to newspaper reports, the seventy-seven-year-old Wallace turned to his beloved wife, and with his last words, said, "I am ready to meet my Maker." He then lapsed into unconsciousness and died at 9:10 p.m. on February 15, 1905. The Wallace family released a statement to newspapers reading: "He fought the good fight and died, as he had lived, without fear."

Reporting on Wallace's death, the *Indianapolis News* praised the former soldier, author, and diplomat as a gallant person who did much to honor Indiana. "He lived as he was born and died as he lived," the *News* said, "a gentleman clean to the bone."

A large number of mourners came to pay their respects to the Hoosier hero, who lay in state at his study. So many came that the Wallace family had to lengthen the time allowed to view the body. Survivors of the Montgomery Guards stood around Wallace's red-cedar coffin. Draped over the casket was the regimental flag given to Wallace by the ladies of Evansville during the Civil War. On his breast he wore the decoration given to him by the sultan, and nearby stood the last page (number 699) he had written of his autobiography.

Around the casket were other souvenirs from his life, including images of his father and mother, a note written by Abraham Lincoln, and Wallace's violin and his wife's guitar, tied together by cloth from Susan's wedding dress.

Family members laid Wallace to rest at Oak Hill Cemetery in Crawfordsville. His grave there is marked by a thirty-foot-tall granite obelisk that includes a carved flag draped over its top. On the marker is inscribed a quote from *Ben-Hur* reading: "I would not give one hour of life as a Soul for a thousand years of life as a man."

Chapter 9

Lew Wallace and *Ben-Hur*

In an 1887 letter to his wife, Susan, Lew Wallace told her that he looked to her and *Ben-Hur* "to keep me unforgotten after the end of life." Susan did all she could to honor her husband's wishes. With the help of Mary Hannah Krout, another Crawfordsville writer, she completed Wallace's unfinished autobiography and saw it through to publication. Susan had to use letters and other material to cover her husband's life from the retreat at the Battle of Monocacy in 1864 to Wallace's death in 1905.

Harper and Brothers released the two-volume book in 1906. The autobiography received its greatest applause from Oliver Howard, the biographer of Zachary Taylor, the man Wallace had worked so strongly against years earlier for his supposed unjust charges of cowardice against Hoosier troops in the Mexican War. Howard lavishly praised Wallace's book as one that "no library or home in our land or any other land can afford to be without."

Susan Wallace treasured her husband's memory. She noted in a letter nine months before her own death that compared to Lew Wallace "all other men are as shadow—and though I look through all the faces on earth I shall never see another like that of my only love." Susan died in Crawfordsville on October 1, 1907.

Others in Indiana continued to honor Lew Wallace. Just days after his death, newspapers around the state were writing that he should be the second person from Indiana to be rewarded with a sculpture in the National Statuary Hall at the U.S. Capitol in Washington, D.C. Established by Congress in 1864, Statuary Hall allowed each state to honor two deceased persons who were known for their "historic renown or for distinguished civic or military services."

In 1900 Indiana had placed its first figure in Statuary Hall, a sculpture of Oliver P. Morton, the state's governor during the Civil War. Although Benjamin Harrison and Thomas Hendricks were considered as possibilities for the state's second statue, Wallace became the popular choice. The state legislature appropriated $5,000 for the Wallace statue, to be carved from Carrara marble by Andrew O'Connor of Paris, France.

The seven-foot-tall statue, the only one honoring a novelist

FROM THE LOCAL HISTORY COLLECTIONS OF THE CRAWFORDSVILLE DISTRICT PUBLIC LIBRARY, INDIANA

Wallace is joined by his grandson, Lew Wallace Jr. (left), and son, Henry Lane Wallace. Henry Lane Wallace served as his father's business manager for many years and continued to look over the author's estate after his death.

136

(Clockwise from top left) Sculptor Andrew O'Connor was the artist responsible for the statue of Wallace displayed at the National Statuary Hall at the U.S. Capitol in Washington, D.C.; O'Connor examines his work on the Wallace statue at his studio in Paris, France; the Wallace statue at Statuary Hall has on its base the words: "Soldier, Author, Diplomat"; a large crowd gathers for the unveiling of the Wallace figure at Statuary Hall.

to be placed in the hall, was unveiled in a ceremony held in Washington on January 11, 1910. Lew Wallace Jr., the author's grandson, pulled the drape that covered the statue. The ceremony also featured a poem in Wallace's honor by James Whitcomb Riley and speeches by such notable Hoosier politicians as Thomas Marshall and Albert Beveridge. Today a bronze copy of the statue stands on the grounds of the Wallace study in Crawfordsville.

Although Wallace had been famous enough to have several schools named in his honor in Indiana, his memory endures today, however, thanks to *Ben-Hur*, a book that has never been out of print. The book's popularity has been helped through the years by stage and film productions.

While he was still alive, Wallace received many requests to turn his best-selling work into a play. He resisted such attempts,

A poster advertising Klaw and Erlanger's play Ben-Hur *at the Illlinois Theatre in Chicago.*

Actor Ramón Novarro as Ben-Hur strains on the oars in a Roman slave galley during the 1925 silent-film version of the novel. The son of a successful Mexican dentist, Novarro first won Hollywood fame in the 1922 movie The Prisoner of Zenda.

Novarro as Ben-Hur (center, left) and Francis X. Bushman as Messala (center, right) are held back from one another before their famous chariot race.

however, fearing that no production could accurately portray Jesus Christ or the exciting chariot race.

In 1899 Wallace reached an agreement with Marc Klaw and Abraham Erlanger, owners of a theatrical syndicate, to turn his novel into a play. The men agreed that Christ would not be played by an actor, but would only be represented by a beam of light. The question of how to hold a chariot race on stage was solved by having horses run on treadmills built into the floor while the scenery moved behind them. Seeing the elaborate sets constructed for the stage version of his novel moved Wallace to exclaim: "My God! Did I set all of this in motion?"

The play opened on November 29, 1899, at the Broadway Theater in New York City. Although the play received mixed reviews, audiences were thrilled and filled seats for every performance. In addition to its successful run on Broadway, the play traveled throughout the country and in Europe and Australia as well. People who had never before been to the theater—especially those with strong religious beliefs who had viewed such productions before as wicked—flocked to see *Ben-Hur*. By the time of its last performance in 1921, an estimated twenty million people had seen the play.

Ben-Hur seemed like the perfect match for America's newest craze in the early twentieth century—motion pictures. Spurred on by such inventors as America's Thomas Edison and France's Auguste and Louis Lumière, motion pictures, or movies, had become a popular form of entertainment by the early 1900s. In 1907 a company called Kalem produced a short film based on *Ben-Hur*. The company, however, had not received permission for doing the film from either the book's publishers or Wallace's family.

Learning of the film, Wallace's son Henry, joined by Harper and Brothers and Klaw and Erlanger, sued Kalem for violating the book's copyright. The case went all the way to the U.S. Supreme Court. In 1911 the Court ruled in favor of Wallace and ordered Kalem to pay $25,000 in damages plus expenses. The case set a precedent for future filmmakers who wanted to turn books into feature films.

The Kalem incident may have soured Henry Wallace's view of movies. Although he received offers for years to sell the rights to his father's work for films, he refused. "I will oppose in every way possible all attempts to produce any of General Wallace's works in moving pictures," he said. "The reason is because the average moving picture shows are wretched exhibitions utterly unworthy of dignified consideration."

Henry Wallace's opinion on the film industry changed in 1915 after seeing D. W. Griffith's *The Birth of a Nation*. The three-hour-long silent film thrilled audiences with its elaborate story and dramatic depiction of America following the Civil War. At first, Henry sought a million dollars for the rights to film *Ben-Hur*. He finally reached an agreement with Erlanger for the then-unheard of sum of $600,000.

The right to film the book was obtained by the Hollywood film company Metro-Goldwyn-Mayer. Although filming on the movie started in Italy, skyrocketing costs caused MGM to move the picture to California. The film starred Ramón Novarro as Ben-Hur and Francis X. Bushman as Messala. Thousands of extras were used in the film, including such Hollywood stars of the time as Lillian Gish, Mary Pickford, Douglas Fairbanks, and Harold Lloyd. The movie ended up costing MGM $3.9 million, making it the most expensive silent film in history.

The film opened to glowing reviews on December 30, 1925, at the George M. Cohan Theater in New York City. Audiences were thrilled by the movie, especially the ship fight between the Romans and the pirates (actually filmed on the sea near Livorno, Italy) and the dramatic chariot race involving Ben-Hur and Messala. A total of forty-two cameras were used to film the chariot race. To add realism to the race, the film's director, Fred Niblo, offered cash prizes to the drivers who finished first, second, and third. Although none of the stuntmen were injured in the dangerous undertaking, several horses were killed in a crash.

The timeless quality of Wallace's *Ben-Hur* caused MGM to turn to it again in the 1950s when the Hollywood studio found itself in a fierce competition with a new form of entertainment—television. Hoping to attract people from their television sets at home back into movie theaters, MGM decided to film a new version of *Ben-Hur*.

The studio picked William Wyler, who had worked on the original 1925 film, to direct and selected Charlton Heston to

COURTESY, THE LILLY LIBRARY, INDIANA UNIVERSITY, BLOOMINGTON, INDIANA

Cameras shot approximately fifty thousand feet of film to capture the chariot race in the 1925 film version of Wallace's novel.

portray the Jewish nobleman Ben-Hur and Stephen Boyd to appear as his boyhood friend and rival Messala. American actors played most of the Jewish roles in the film, while Wyler picked British actors to portray the Roman characters.

MGM had a lot riding on the film. Heston noted that if the movie failed to attract customers, the studio might have gone bankrupt. MGM officials, however, were confident that *Ben-Hur* could outdo what the epic *The Ten Commandments*, which had starred Heston as Moses, had done at the box office. "There aren't more than half the Commandments you could call really interesting," said one MGM official. "We figure we've got a superior story."

Wyler, a three-time Academy Award winner, shot the movie

on location near Rome, Italy, over a nine-month period. Heston and Boyd were trained to drive the four-horse team and chariots by veteran stuntman Yakim Canutt. Thousands of extras were on hand on a set designed to resemble the Roman Circus to cheer as Heston and Boyd, who did most of their own stunts, battled as Ben-Hur and Messala. "Thundering past those screaming extras over the finish line was as thrilling as anything I've done in pictures," said Heston. He called the chariot race "arguably the best action scene ever filmed." In this case, none of the stuntmen or horses received serious injuries during the race.

When he finished filming on January 7, 1959, Wyler had shot a million feet of film and spent $15 million, the most expensive movie ever made at that time. MGM had used its money wisely. "Ben-Hur turned out to be all we hoped for," said Heston.

The nearly four-hour movie premiered to glowing reviews from most critics on November 18, 1959, at the Lowe's State Theatre in New York City. The film went on to earn more than $40 million. At the 1960 Academy Award ceremony, *Ben-Hur* became the first film ever to win eleven Academy Awards, a mark later matched by the 1998 movie *Titanic*. Heston won the Oscar for Best Actor and Wyler captured the statuette for Best Director.

Over the years, the 1959 *Ben-Hur* has continued to thrill and inspire viewers through its frequent broadcasts on television. In 1998 the American Film Institute named *Ben-Hur* as one of the hundred greatest American movies of all time. Heston, who went on to star in such legendary films as *The Agony and the Ecstasy* and *Planet of the Apes*, called his performance as Wallace's noble Ben-Hur his "best film work."

Ben-Hur's fame lives on today. It has been used as the name for towns, for such products as bicycles and candy, and for a variety of businesses. What is often ignored, however, is the person who created the character—Lew Wallace. His role in the history of Indiana

Actor Charlton Heston as Ben-Hur strains to control his chariot during the 1959 Ben-Hur. More than fifteen thousand extras were used for the chariot race scene.

GETTY IMAGES

and of the country, however, should not be forgotten. Wallace's life touched upon key events and figures in the United States, from pioneer days to the Civil War and the age of the automobile to this country's rise to prominence in the early twentieth century.

Through all the turmoil and upheaval of a country experiencing its own growing pains, Wallace remembered who he was and where he came from. Wherever duty took him, Wallace always managed to find his way back to the comforts and familiar surroundings of his Hoosier home. But he was never afraid to follow his dreams. "Men speak of dreaming as if it were a phenomenon of night and sleep," Wallace said. "They should know better. Living is dreaming. Only in the grave are there no dreams."

Learn More *about* Wallace

Upon his death, Lew Wallace left behind a treasure trove of letters, speeches, and souvenirs of his life. Two libraries in Indiana have gathered together much of what Wallace left behind and have made his work available for researchers and the public.

The Lilly Library at Indiana University in Bloomington has a number of Wallace's original manuscripts, including his most famous work, *Ben-Hur*. The Indiana Historical Society's William Henry Smith Memorial Library in Indianapolis has a large collection of Wallace's papers, including letters from his service during the Civil War, his days as governor of the New Mexico Territory, and his service as U.S. minister to Turkey.

Two of Indiana's most famous authors: Lew Wallace (left) and James Whitcomb Riley.

148

IUS. INDIANAPOLIS-MARION COUNTY PUBLIC LIBRARY RILEY COLLECTION, C6048

The Indiana Historical Society is also sponsoring the publication of a microfilm edition of all the known letters and writings of Wallace and his wife, Susan. In addition, the Wallace Papers will include the author's manuscripts and photographs and drawings taken by and of the Wallaces. The project is scheduled for completion in 2006.

Wallace wrote about his life in two volumes of memoirs, titled *Lew Wallace: An Autobiography* (New York: Harper and Brothers, 1906). There have also been two complete biographies written about the Hoosier general and author. The first was written by Irving McKee and is titled *"Ben-Hur" Wallace: The Life of General Lew Wallace* (Berkeley: University of California Press, 1947). A more complete picture of Wallace's life is presented in Robert E. and Katharine M. Morsberger's book *Lew Wallace: Militant Romantic* (New York: McGraw-Hill, 1980). Wallace is one of five Hoosier writers highlighted in Barbara Olenyik Morrow's book *From* Ben-Hur *to* Sister Carrie: *Remembering the Lives and Works of Five Indiana Authors* (Indianapolis: Guild Press of Indiana, 1995).

More about Wallace's days as the commander of the Eleventh Indiana Infantry in the Civil War can be found in Jeffrey L. Patrick, ed., *Three Years with Wallace's Zouaves: The Civil War Memoirs of Thomas Wise Durham* (Macon, GA: Mercer University Press, 2003). Wallace's experience in the Battle of Shiloh is explored in James Lee McDonough's *Shiloh—in Hell before Night* (Knoxville: The University of Tennessee Press, 1977). Wallace's stand at the Battle of Monocacy is a major part of Frank E. Vandiver's book *Jubal's Raid: General Early's Famous Attack on Washington in 1864* (Lincoln: University of Nebraska Press, 1988).

The assassination of Abraham Lincoln and the court trial that followed involving the Lincoln conspirators is covered in such books as James L. Swanson and Daniel R. Weinberg's *Lincoln's Assassins: Their Trial and Execution* (Sante Fe, NM: Arena Editions, 2001) and Michael W. Kauffman's *American Brutus: John Wilkes Booth and the Lincoln Conspiracies* (New York: Random House, 2004).

Western historian Robert M. Utley has written two well-regarded books about Wallace's time as governor of the New Mexico Territory. They are *High Noon in Lincoln: Violence on the Western Frontier* (Albuquerque: University of New Mexico Press, 1987) and *Billy the Kid: A Short and Violent Life* (Lincoln: University of Nebraska Press, 1989). For this period in history, another good source is William A. Keleher's book *Violence in Lincoln County, 1861–1881* (Albuquerque: University of New Mexico Press, 1957).

A number of articles have been written about the different activities Wallace worked at during his life. These include the following:

Ray E. Boomhower, "Major General Lew Wallace: Savior of Washington, D.C.," *Traces of Indiana and Midwestern History* (Winter 1993).

John D. Forbes, "Lew Wallace, Romantic," *Indiana Magazine of History* (December 1948).

Oakah L. Jones, "Lew Wallace: Hoosier Governor of Territorial New Mexico, 1878–81," *New Mexico Historical Review* (April 1985).

Irving McKee, "The Early Life of Lew Wallace," *Indiana Magazine of History* (September 1941).

Robert Ryal Miller, "Lew Wallace and the French Intervention in Mexico," *Indiana Magazine of History* (March 1963).

Gail M. Stephens, "Lew Wallace's Fall from Grace," *North & South* (May 2004). [About Wallace and his Civil War days, especially the Battle of Shiloh.]

Lee Scott Theisen, "'The Land of Sudden Death,' Governor Lew Wallace of New Mexico, 1878–1881," *Smoke Signals* (Spring 1980).

Donald E. Thompson, "Lew Wallace and *Ben-Hur*," *Indiana Libraries* (1988).

James A. Treichel, "Lew Wallace at Fort Donelson," *Indiana Magazine of History* (March 1963).

Robert M. Utley, "Who was Billy the Kid?" *Montana Magazine of Western History* (Summer 1987).

Vernon L. Volpe, "'Dispute Every Inch of Ground': Major General Lew Wallace Commands Cincinnati, September, 1862," *Indiana Magazine of History* (1989).

Harold Lew Wallace, "Lew Wallace's March to Shiloh Revisted," *Indiana Magazine of History* (March 1963).

Wallace sits at his desk surrounded by his books inside his study at Crawfordsville.

FROM THE LOCAL HISTORY COLLECTIONS OF THE CRAWFORDSVILLE DISTRICT PUBLIC LIBRARY, INDIANA

Wallace Historic Sites

The following historic sites will lead the reader to a broader understanding of some of the most important experiences in Lew Wallace's life. If you plan on making a visit to one of these places, please call, write, or visit their Web sites for the most up-to-date information.

General Lew Wallace Study and Museum is located in Wallace's private study at 200 Wallace Avenue in Crawfordsville, Indiana. The museum is owned by the city of Crawfordsville and is operated by the Parks and Recreation Department. In the study are numerous items collected by Wallace during his life. Admission is $3 for adults, $1 for students, and free for those six years and under. For more information and hours of operation, call the museum at (765) 362-5769 or visit its Web site at http://www.ben-hur.com.

Shiloh National Military Park is located in Hardin County, on the west bank of the Tennessee River, about nine miles south of Savannah, Tennessee. The 4,000-acre battlefield preserves the scene of the two-day battle between Confederate and Union armies on April 6 and 7, 1862. Within the park's boundaries are also the Shiloh National Cemetery and prehistoric Indian mounds. Admission is $5 for a single private vehicle. The park's visitor center is open from 8 a.m. to 5 p.m. daily. For visitor information, call (731) 689-5696 or visit the park's Web site at http://www.nps.gov/shil/.

Monocacy National Battlefield is located near Frederick, Maryland. The park commemorates the stand made by Union troops against a large force of Confederate soldiers under the command of General Jubal Early. The fight here became known as the "Battle That Saved Washington." The park's Gambrill Mill Visitor Center is open daily Labor Day through Memorial Day from 8 a.m. to 4:30 p.m. and Memorial Day through Labor Day from 8:30 a.m. to 5:00 p.m. Admission is free. For more information, call (301) 662-3515, or visit the park's Web site at http://www.nps.gov/mono/.

Palace of the Governors is a National Historic Landmark located at 120 Washington Avenue in Santa Fe, New Mexico. Originally constructed in the early seventeenth century as Spain's seat of government in what is today the American southwest, the Palace of the Governors is now New Mexico's history museum. Admission is $7 for an adult; those age sixteen and under are admitted free. The

Palace is open from 10 a.m. to 5 p.m. Tuesday through Sunday. For more information, visit the Palace Web site at http://www.palaceofthegovernors.org/.

Index

50, 53; removed from command, 7, 66; and writing, 8–9, 11, 12, 21, 24, 25, 26, 34, 41, 89–91, 108, 110, 125–26, 129; love of books and reading, 8, 16, 19, 23; and Mexico, 8, 80–81, 87–89; serves on court that tries Lincoln conspirators, 8, 81–83; as governor of New Mexico Territory, 8, 97–111; as minister to Turkey, 8, 112, 115–24; death of, 12, 133–34; birth, 13; describes his father, 14; and love of fishing, 15; has scarlet fever, 15; and memories of his mother, 16; and wanderlust, 16, 17, 19, 21, 23; disciplined by parents, 16, 18, 22; and stepmother, 17–18, 19; skips school, 19–20; father cuts off financial support of, 22; joins militia, 25–26; robbed of savings, 34; marries, 35, 39; and violin, 36, 41, 134; fistfight with political opponent, 37; first meeting with Abraham Lincoln, 37–38; birth of son, 41; victim of confidence man, 41–42; on slavery and abolitionists, 42, 44; and politics, 42, 45, 89, 95–98, 119, 121; draws Lincoln conspirators (illus.), 82–83; serves on Wirz commission, 85–87; resigns from army, 87; gifts from Sultan, 122, 124 ,130, 134; and the study, 124, 126, 128–29; oversees vote count in disputed 1876 presidential election, 95; autobiography, 129, 133, 134, 135; encourages young authors, 130, 132; statue of, 136, 138 (illus.), 137; (illus.) opposite 1, 10, 31, 35, 40, 49, 59, 74, 94, 99, 119, 120, 123, 124, 128, 131, 132, 133, 136, 148, 152

Wallace, Lew Jr. (Lew's grandson) 138; (illus.), 10, 128, 136

Wallace, Susan Arnold Elston, 8, 35, 39, 41, 53, 65, 93, 105, 106, 110, 113, 119, 121, 122, 126 133, 134, 135, 136; (illus.), 35, 44

Wallace, W. H. L., 61

Wallace, William, 16

Wallace, William (Lew's brother), 16, 17, 22, 26, 30, 37, 75, 130

Wallace, Zerelda Gray Sanders (Lew's stepmother), 17, 19; (illus.), 17

Walnut Springs, 30, 32

War of 1812, p. 7

Washington, D.C., 8, 9, 55, 66, 69, 70, 71, 72, 73, 77, 80, 81, 91, 104, 111, 112, 136

Welles, Gideon, 81

West Point, 2–3, 7, 14, 25, 50, 53, 65

Whig Party, 14, 19, 20, 34

White, Charles, 41

Whitman, Walt, 83

Wilson, John B., 103

Wirz, Henry, 84, 86, 87

Woman's Christian Temperance Union, 17

World Columbian Exposition, 126

Wyler, William, 142, 143, 144

Yildiz Kiosk, 116

Zouaves, 4, 44, 48, 52; (illus.), 51